"You can't force me to stay here. You have no right."

"You are not leaving here," Leo interrupted. "I brought you here to protect you, and that is what I am going to do."

"Protect me?" she protested. "Is that what you call it? Invading a girl's bedroom—"

"Be careful what you say, Phoebe," he cut in ruthlessly, "or I will be forced to remind you just how willing a bed partner you were." His hand touched her cheek and stroked back to tangle in her hair. "And you will be again."

JACQUELINE BAIRD began writing as a hobby when her family objected to the smell of her oil painting, and immediately became hooked on romance. She loves traveling, and worked her way around the world from Europe to the Americas and Australia, returning to marry her teenage sweetheart. Jacqueline and husband Jim live in Northumbria, England, and they have two grown sons.

Books by Jacqueline Baird

JACQUELINE BAIRD

The Reluctant Fiancée

Harlequin Books

TORONTO • NEW YORK • LONDON
AMSTERDAM • PARIS • SYDNEY • HAMBURG
STOCKHOLM • ATHENS • TOKYO • MILAN
MADRID • WARSAW • BUDAPEST • AUCKLAND

ISBN 0-373-11942-9

THE RELUCTANT FIANCÉE

First North American Publication 1998.

Printed in U.S.A.

CHAPTER ONE

BEA looked around the crowded room, her full lips twitching in a wry grimace. Music blared from two amplifiers, gyrating bodies were everywhere and the flashing lights were giving her a headache. She should be enjoying herself; after all she was in *her* living room! It was *her* twenty-first birthday party! *Her* friends!

She turned her back on the crowd and stared out of the tall Georgian window to the blackness beyond. Bea lifted a fluted champagne glass to her mouth and took a sip of the bubbly. It was as flat as she felt. It was futile to worry, she knew, but she did not seem to be able to help it.

Tomorrow she was travelling down to London, and on Monday she would start work as a junior partner in the firm of Stephen-Gregoris, an import and export firm started forty years ago by her late father, John Stephen, and his greek Cypriot friend, Nick Gregoris. But it wasn't the thought of work that bothered her, or the fact that the firm had diversified into other areas. No, her real worry was that she would have to meet Leon Gregoris again.

Leon Gregoris was the chairman and managing director, and a despot to boot, as she knew from past experience... Also, until today, he had been the trustee of her thirty per cent share of the business, left to her by her father.

As a child Bea had considered Leon a friend, even though he was fourteen years older than her. But that had ended when her father had died. For the last three years any communication between them had been strictly business, conducted through lawyers and the occasional telephone call.

An orphan at seventeen, Bea had stayed on in the home she had shared with her father in Northumbria. Her mother had died when she was a baby and it was her honorary aunty Lil and her uncle Bob who had looked after her.

They still did. A fond smile curved Bea's full lips. She was going to miss the elderly couple when she was in London. She had never really had to take care of herself before. While attending the University of Newcastle upon Tyne she had simply travelled in every day. Now she was the proud recipient of a first-class degree in Maths and Accountancy, and on Monday she would take her place in her father's firm!

A frown creased her smooth brow. Leon Gregoris was the only fly in the ointment; she cringed at the thought of seeing him, not at all sure of her ability to face up to him.

For heaven's sake! Was she a woman? Or a wimp? She shook her head dismissively. She was bright, intelligent, and no longer the naive eighteen-year-old girl she had been when she had last seen Leon, in love with the idea of love.

'Humph!' she snorted, disgusted with the memory of her much younger, gullible self. 'You're a fool, Bea. You have nothing to worry about,' she told herself firmly, and, lifting her glass, she took another large swallow of champagne, unaware she had spoken out loud.

'If you say so, Phoebe, darling. Far be it from me to disagree with a lady.'

The deep melodious voice made the hair on the back of her neck stand on end. She would have known that voice anywhere. Her hand tightened, white-knuckled, on the stem of her glass. It couldn't be! She raised her eyes and stared at the couple reflected in the window pane.

Her own reflection showed a young woman of average height with straight silver-blonde hair and pale, bare shoulders. She wore a silver Spandex sheath dress that clung to the soft curves of firm breasts and on down to fit like a second skin over feminine hips, ending mid-thigh and exposing long, shapely legs.

All the colour left Bea's face. The picture she presented was almost ghostly, but there was nothing ghost-like about the tall, dark man hovering behind her. Warlock, more like! she thought grimly. Wide shoulders seemed to shadow her. The harsh, handsome features had not changed a jot, she realised, swallowing hard. Too long black wavy hair, and even blacker piercing eyes. Slowly turning around to face him, she silently added, And an even blacker heart...

'You, Leon,' she murmured, finally finding her voice and hating the way it quavered. She tilted her head back and looked up into his tanned, attractive face. He was watching her, laughter lighting his dark eyes. He knew damn well he had shocked her rigid. 'What are you do-ing here?' she demanded curtly. 'I didn't invite you.'

'An oversight on your part, Phoebe, but I forgive you,' he drawled mockingly. 'You know I wouldn't miss your twenty-first birthday for the world.'

He was the only person who ever called her Phoebe, and she hated it. She opened her mouth to tell him as much, but never got the chance. Two large hands settled on her naked shoulders and a firm male mouth descended on her parted lips.

Whatever she had been about to say vanished from her mind at the first touch of his mouth on hers. She closed her eyes.

Bea knew she should resist, and lifted her free hand

to press against the hard wall of his chest, but for some reason her fingers spread out instead, over the soft silk of his shirt.

It was Leon who broke the kiss, murmuring against her mouth, 'Happy birthday, darling.' Then, lifting his head and staring down into her flushed, beautiful face, he winked...

'The chemistry is still fizzing, Phoebe, which is more than can be said for the glass of champagne you're clutching with such tenacity.' And, taking the glass from her unresisting hand, he placed it on the windowsill. 'I'll get you another. Come on.' Capturing her hand, he added, 'Let's get out of here and into the study, where we can talk.'

Bea shook her head to clear her brain. He was doing it again, exactly as he had years ago. Mesmerising her, poor fool, with a kiss, and then ordering her about. That was Leon's *modus operandi* and she would do well to remember it.

'No, thank you, I've had quite enough to drink.' She snatched her hand free. 'And as for talking we can discuss all we need to at our meeting on Monday.' She was proud of her ability to speak firmly to Leon for once, and, bravely meeting his narrowed gaze, she added for good measure, 'But if you would like a drink please help yourself. The bar is in the dining room. You know the way.' Half turning, she would have walked past him, but Leon's hand closed around her upper arm, halting her in her stride.

'Not so fast, Phoebe.'

She fought down the tingling sensation the large hand curved around her flesh aroused, and looked up into his face. 'In case you hadn't noticed, I have guests. I must mingle.'

Black eyes raked her from head to toe in a blatant

sexual appraisal, lingering for a moment on the shadowy cleavage cupped in silver Spandex before returning to her face. 'Mingling with you was actually what I had in mind. How about it, Phoebe?' Leon asked with deliberate provocation, his long fingers caressing the bare skin of her arm. 'Interested?'

Bea looked at the man towering over her and recognised the sensual amusement glittering in his eyes. Leon hadn't changed in three years. He was still as devastatingly attractive as ever, and he knew it. It was there in his arrogant stance, an animal magnetism he exuded without even trying. Add wealth, power and sophistication, and he was a lethal cocktail to any member of the female species.

Tonight he was wearing a conservative business suit, dark navy, with a plain white silk shirt and a muted blue and red striped tie. His jacket was open and pleated trousers hung comfortably on his lean hips. For a second she wondered why he was dressed that way at almost midnight on a Saturday night, at a party he had not been invited to. But she refrained from asking. She simply wanted him out of her house.

'Will I do?' Leon asked, arching one dark eyebrow enquiringly, fully aware that she had been studying him. Bea could feel hot colour flood her cheeks, and was not sure if it was from anger or embarrassment.

'Does your silence mean you're considering my offer, Phoebe, darling?' he teased huskily.

His deep voice was awfully close to her ear, and, jerking her arm free from his hold, she shot back scathingly, 'Still the incorrigible flirt, Leon. I pity your poor wife and...family.' For some reason she could not bring herself to say 'child'. 'How they tolerate your many escapades I can't imagine,' she added, trying for a flippant note, horrified to realise that his touch, his closeness, still had the power to make her go weak at the knees. But there was no way she was going to let him see it. Never again...

He straightened to his full height and stepped back. 'My family, if you can call it a family, is fine. My stepmother and stepsister live in California, and I rarely see them unless they want something.' He stared down at her with eyes as black as jet, all trace of amusement gone. 'As for a wife, you should know the answer to that better than most,' he opined cynically.

'Sorry, I haven't kept up with your private affairs,' she said, drawling out the last word deliberately.

Bea's blue eyes, filled with contempt, flicked up over the hard planes of his face, his smooth, tanned skin, the faint shadow of his square jaw; she saw the sheer animal strength of him, and more. He was furiously angry, but hiding it well. Deciding discretion was called for, unless she wanted a fight in a room full of people, Bea added with a calm she was far from feeling, 'It takes me all my time to keep up to date on our business partnership. Your personal life is your own. Forget I mentioned it.'

'Forget?' Leon smiled, a cynical twist of his hard lips. 'How could I forget, when the nearest I ever got to falling into the matrimonial trap was the abortive engagement you and I shared for a few idyllic months, my sweet Phoebe?'

Idyllic! My eye, she thought bitterly, and, looking anywhere but at Leon, she realised a good percentage of her guests were watching them with avid curiosity. Damn the man! 'I don't know what you want to discuss that can't wait until Monday, but you were right; the study would be better.'

'There now, Phoebe.' A large arm fell across her shoulders and urged her through the press of bodies towards the door. 'I knew you would see it my way in the end.'

Once in the relative peace of the elegant oak-panelled hall, Bea shrugged off Leon's guiding arm. 'I do know where the study is. This is my home.' She mocked him, walking towards the large door to the rear of the sweeping staircase with Leon a step behind her.

'True, but the bird is about to fly the nest at last.' He sighed, with a hint of irritation in his deep voice. 'Which is why we need to talk about your entrance into the wider world of London, and work.'

Bea glanced up at his handsome face; he looked older. A few lines crinkled at the corners of his black eyes, and more bracketed his sensuous mouth. And was that grey she spied in the thick black hair swept back behind his ear? Yet he could still have wowed the whole of the feminine population. Inexplicably she felt a sudden tenderness sweep through her for the man—after all, he had been a good friend once. Maybe they could be friends again.

Leon's long arm reached over her head and pushed open the panelled study door. He stood aside for her to enter. Bea walked in and breathed deeply. She loved this room, and even after all this time she still imagined the spirit of her father lingered in the air. It was a library-cum-study—a room where the man of the house could relax.

'I always loved this room,' Leon remarked, glancing about him appreciatively, and then, closing and locking the heavy door behind him, he gestured towards the sofa. 'Sit down.'

Bea seated herself stiffly on the edge of the sofa and tried not to look as nervous as she felt. 'So what is it that's so vital it can't wait until Monday?' she said in a rush. Suddenly being alone in a locked room with Leon seemed vaguely threatening. Bea watched as he strolled past her to lean one arm on the mantelpiece, tall, elegant and completely at ease, while her own nerves were stretched to breaking point.

'You are extraordinarily like your mother,' he remarked, ignoring her question, his glance flicking to fix intently upon her. His dark eyes slid over her with the sensual thoroughness of a professional womaniser. 'You have grown into an incredibly attractive woman, but then I always knew you would.'

'Really, Leon, if you've brought me in here to practise your chat-up lines, forget it... I'm immune to your brand of charm,' she lied, with a hint of mockery in her voice. 'Been there, done that, worn the tee-shirt.'

'Not strictly true, darling. I never actually did it with you,' he shot back, his sensuous mouth curved in a mocking smile. 'But who knows? I might oblige you some time, if you ask me nicely.'

Bea's colour deepened at the sexist comment, but she said nothing. Leon was the most extraordinary man she had ever known. He made no secret of what he wanted from a woman and yet he had them queuing up to share his bed. But she was determined not to be added to his long list of conquests. She'd had a lucky escape three years ago, and she needed to keep reminding herself of the fact.

'I'll take your silence as a compliment and live in hope,' Leon chuckled, and, after straightening up, in two lithe strides he was beside her. 'You're right, of course. I really do not have time for flirtation at the minute.' Dropping onto a sofa, he half turned to face her, suddenly all business. 'The company jet is waiting for me at Newcastle airport. I have to be in New York tomorrow, hence the detour to see you.'

Bea stared at him. 'You're incredible.' She shook her head in amazement.

'I know, Phoebe,' he drawled, with an element of seduction in his deep voice. He couldn't help himself, Bea thought wryly, fighting to suppress a grin.

'But enough about me. It is you we have to concentrate on. I will not be in the London office for at least the next two weeks, which presents me with something of a dilemma. I did want to be there for your first day with the company, but it is simply not possible. However, I have talked to Tom Jordan and everything is organised for your arrival. But first...' Slipping his hand into his inside jacket pocket, he withdrew a document and a pen. 'The reason for my whistlestop visit. Your official entry into the adult world.' Placing the parchment paper on her knee, he indicated where she was to sign. 'As of midnight tonight my trusteeship ends and you are the outright owner of thirty per cent of the company. Free and clear.'

'Oh! I see.' Taking the pen, she scribbled her signature where he indicated. So he had not called simply because it was her birthday, and now the conservative suit made sense. For a brief moment Bea felt a swift stab of something very like disappointment. She quickly dismissed the notion. Good heavens! It was a relief, surely, that she would not have to be around Leon. Hadn't she been dreading the thought of meeting him only half an hour ago? But as he continued speaking her relief was overtaken by a rising anger.

'I have arranged with Tom Jordan, the manager of the London office, for you to start work as an assistant to his PA, Margot. You'll like her, she's a great woman, and she knows almost as much as Tom about the workings of the office. Another plus—she also has an apartment in the same building where your father used to live

when he was in town. I take it you will be using your
father's apartment? So you will not be alone at all.
You'll have a friend—'

'Wait just a minute,' Bea interrupted angrily. At another time she might have found the startled expression
in his dark eyes amusing, but right now she was too
furious. 'As of now I own a large slice of Stephen-
Gregoris.' Shoving the document back at him to emphasise her point, she continued, 'And as such I have no
intention of starting work as an assistant to somebody
else's personal assistant. I have not spent the last three
years of my life studying to end up as some office junior.
I am no longer the little girl you knew. I am an intelligent woman who intends to take an active part in my
late father's company. Junior partner, yes... Anything
else, I don't want to know.'

Her blue eyes, glittering with anger, flicked over his
impassive countenance, and then wildly around the
room. 'Put that in your pipe and smoke it, Mr Leon
Gregoris,' she quipped, probably because her glance had
caught her father's pipestand, she realised. And instantly
she wished she could take the childish words back. But
she could not believe the cheek of the man... No discussion, no asking her opinion—typical Leon. Do this!
Live there! Have this friend!

'So the kitten has developed claws,' Leon said softly,
and, slipping the document into his pocket, he turned
more fully to face her. But his eyes narrowed to slits of
anger when he saw her furious blue gaze resting on him.
'Damn it, Phoebe, don't be so stupid. There is no way
a girl of twenty-one, however brilliant, can walk into a
company as a partner. I run the business, and I have
made you a wealthy woman in the process. Content
yourself with that. In fact you don't need to work at all.
But, if you must, it has got to be the way I say.'

'No way,' she spat back.

His hands snaked out and tightened around her slender wrists, and she felt the pressure of his fingers biting into her flesh. Her pulse raced, but with anger, not passion, she told herself. She looked into his hard face and recognised the resolute expression there, but she refused to be intimidated by it.

'My way. Understand?' he said tersely.

'Oh, yes, I understand very well, Leon. Keep little Phoebe in her place or she's out of the business altogether. So you can remain the absolute dictator, the tyrant you have always been. My God! You were even prepared to marry me once, simply to keep your all-powerful position, until I wised up to what you were after.' As soon as the words left her mouth she knew she had gone too far.

His black eyes widened in astonishment, and then narrowed in anger as the import of what she had said registered in his astute brain. 'You little bitch!' he exclaimed. 'At last the truth is coming out. You broke our engagement not because I was too old—your desertion had nothing to do with my age,' Leon snarled, and, jerking at her hands, he dragged her across his lap. 'You actually thought I was trying to control your share of the company. You simply did not trust me.'

He'd got that right! Bea thought, and almost laughed at the incredulous expression in his dark eyes. But her own position was far from safe, so she bit down any response.

'My God, I should give you the good hiding you deserve. But, as you were at pains to point out, you're a woman now.' Twisting her around, he pushed her flat on her back on the sofa. 'A more adult punishment is called for.'

Confusion replaced her earlier anger and she could

hear the thunder of her own heartbeat. She saw his expression as he bent over her. 'No!' she cried, and then his face became a twisted blur as his hand tangled in her long hair and his hard mouth fastened on hers in a long, grinding kiss.

Bea fought against him with all the strength she possessed. Her small hands pushed at his mighty shoulders, and when that had no effect she dug her fingers into the nape of his neck. He retaliated by rearing back. With his free hand he grasped the front of her dress, and in a second it was down around her waist and his hand was clasping one firm breast.

She gasped, and, taking full advantage of her parted lips, his mouth covered hers again, his tongue plunging into its sweet, dark cavern. His full weight came down on top of her and long fingers nipped the perfect bud of her breast, teasing it into hard, pulsing life. Electric sensations shuddered through her even as she bucked beneath him, trying to throw him off. But she was no match for his superior size and strength, and, worse, when his kisses changed to a tempting fiery passion, she was helpless to resist.

His mouth never left hers but his hands were everywhere, stroking, teasing, tormenting. His muscled leg moved over her thigh and she felt the full pressure of his masculine arousal hard against her flesh... Her *flesh*!

Her passion-dulled mind came alive to what was happening. The lamé dress was now little more than a belt around her waist, and alarm returned to give her the motivation to fight. She lifted her hand and deliberately raked her long nails down the side of his face.

'What the hell—?' As he reared back she took her chance and slid from under him onto the floor. She didn't care what she looked like, and, struggling to her knees, she hauled up the front of her dress, then stood up and tugged down the skirt.

She backed away from where he sat rubbing his hand against his cheek. Her breasts heaving and her face flushed, she watched him warily. He looked down in amazement at the blood on his hand, and then back up to fix Bea with glittering black eyes.

'You little vixen. You drew blood!'

'Serves you right—you attacked me.' She had no idea how aroused or how young she looked to the seated man, or how beautiful. She was still reeling from the totally unexpected explosion of passion between them, and her own shameful reaction to Leon.

For a long moment they simply stared at each other, the sexual tension in the air almost tangible.

Leon finally broke the contact. He looked down at the floor and said quietly, 'Yes, I did, and I apologise.'

Bea's bewildered blue eyes searched his handsome face; Leon apologising was unheard of. 'You apologise?' she queried, as if she didn't believe what she was hearing.

'Yes, a hundred times over.' He glanced at her with a look in his eyes that she could not fathom. 'I am a lot older than you and I should have more control. But in all the years we have known each other it never once entered my head that you did not trust me.'

Bea, for some unknown reason, found it hard to look him in the eye. Yet he had made no attempt to deny her accusation. So why did she feel ashamed? It was Leon who should be ashamed, for having tried to trick a grieving teenager. But she doubted he knew the meaning of the word 'ashamed'. Leon moved through life supremely confident of his own abilities, a ruthless predator, cutthroat in business, overpowering the opposition with arrogant ease. And, Bea realised, he was just as ruthless in his private life.

He shrugged his broad shoulders, dismissing the question of trust, and ran his hands through his dishevelled hair, sweeping it back from his brow. 'Also, Phoebe, I should have explained in more detail your position in the company.' He glanced at the slim gold Rolex on his wrist and grimaced.

'I was in too much of a hurry. But please try and understand, you will not be working as the office junior. Tom and Margot have strict instructions to show you every aspect of the London office and how the company works. You will get to know all the staff we employ there personally. Your job description as a PAA is modest enough, so they will not resent you. But if you insist on walking in and declaring you're a part owner, and also insist on starting as a junior partner, there is bound to be resentment. Do you want that? The snide remarks about nepotism at work? Perhaps even publicity in the press?'

Bea had not thought about it from that angle, but she realised Leon had a valid point. 'No, no, I don't,' she said quietly.

'I didn't think you would. That is why I made the arrangements I did. Only Tom and Margot know your true status in the company, but it is up to you if you want to tell everyone else. Personally, I only wanted to give you some protection, at least for your first few months in a working environment. I had hoped to be able to stay in England for a few weeks, but it simply is not possible.

'Branching out into the USA and the Far East in the past few years has been a great success, but I seem to spend most of my time jetting between New York, Hong Kong and Athens—as you must know by the company reports you receive.' He glanced at her, black eyes capturing blue. 'You do read them?' he asked with a smile, and her heart gave a curious lurch in her chest at the sight of it.

'Yes, of course.' She smiled back and took a step towards him. Leon was right. Since taking over the company he had expanded its business enormously. It had been successfully floated on the London Stock Exchange, but their two families still retained sixty per cent of the shares, thus ensuring that it remained a family concern. Leon's name was regularly featured in the financial newspapers all over the world, and the meteoric rise of Stephen-Gregoris as a leading international company was constantly remarked upon. As for the tabloid newspapers, they had nicknamed him the "Swashbuckling Tycoon"—probably because when he'd first come to their notice, in his mid-twenties, he'd worn his hair in a ponytail.

'You're right,' she admitted. 'It was stupid of me to think I could walk into the firm as a partner. I realise that now. But I do want to learn everything, and perhaps eventually I can visit the overseas offices too, maybe even work in one.' The more she thought about it, the more she liked the idea. 'Maybe this time next year it will be me going to New York.'

'Why not?' Leon stood up and, crossing to where she stood, once more took her hands in his. 'Next week London, next year the world.'

Bea tilted her head back to look up into his face, her expression serious. 'Are you teasing, or do you really think I can do it?' she asked, in a voice that was surprisingly calm considering the way the pulses in her wrists were racing beneath his fingers.

He released her hands and dropped a swift kiss on the

top of her head. 'I think, Phoebe, you will do whatever you set your mind to, and the world had better look out.'

'You as well.' She grinned up at him, mischief dancing in her eyes. 'I might decide I want your job.'

Leon's mouth twitched, and then he chuckled. 'You're some woman, Phoebe.' He shook his dark head, still smiling. 'But I really must be going.' Withdrawing a small velvet box from his trouser pocket, he dropped it into her hand. 'Happy birthday, and good luck on Monday. I'll be in touch.' Turning, he started for the door.

'Wait. I'll see you out.' She hurried after him, but he stopped her with a hand on her shoulder.

'Not a good idea, Phoebe, unless you want your friends to get the wrong idea.'

'My friends?' He had lost her; she didn't know what he meant.

'Have a look in the mirror before mingling again, darling...' Leon drawled softly, and after unlocking the door he went, his laughter ringing in her ears.

Standing where Leon had left her, Bea slowly opened the box. Inside was a delicate pendant, a deep blue sapphire surrounded by diamonds, ringed in gold and suspended on a gold chain. After fastening the chain around her neck, she picked up the pendant and gazed at it in wonder. Leon was an incredibly generous but infuriating man.

CHAPTER TWO

STILL bemused by Leon's present, Bea wondered why he had not stopped to see her open it. What had he said? 'Look in the mirror!' Bea mumbled to herself, quietly slipping out of the study. She quickly dived into the cloakroom—luckily free.

One look in the mirror above the vanity basin, and the pendant was forgotten. Instead she wanted to die of shame. Her blonde hair was a tangled mess around her face—a very flushed face—and the remains of once red lipgloss were smeared over her skin, but none of it on her lips—lips that were unmistakably swollen. Worse, the dress she had hastily pulled up after escaping from Leon on the sofa clung decorously over one breast, then slanted down over the other, revealing the dark areola around her nipple to the world.

Bea groaned out loud. Never again would she wear the silver Spandex creation, she vowed. No wonder Leon had told her to look in the mirror. But the swine could have told her earlier about the dress, instead of feasting his eyes and having a good laugh at her expense. To think she had actually been considering they could be friends again!

Splashing her face with cold water, and tidying herself up as best she could, she felt a humourless laugh escape her. Would she never learn where Leon was concerned? He had arrived, got her to agree to what he wanted, and left... As for her birthday present, to a man of Leon's wealth, the pendant was a mere trinket.

She knew she was being irrational. She was a very

wealthy woman herself. But somehow she never thought of herself as such. Her parents, because they'd been from the north, had always lived there, though her father often stayed in London. As a child Bea had known they were comfortably off, but never thought much about it. And since Leon had taken over the running of the company, and then since the death of her father, she hadn't liked to think how much she was worth. It seemed indecent when she had done nothing for it. Which was another reason for her going to work in London. She felt it her duty...

Two o'clock in the morning, and she leant against the front doorframe, grateful for the breath of cool air and the support. She was dead beat. With a sigh of relief she closed the door, locked and bolted it. At last she was alone...

The caterers had cleaned up and left ten minutes earlier. Aunty Lil and Uncle Bob would have nothing to complain about when they arrived back in the morning from their night out in the city. She hoped they'd had a better time than she'd had...

Some party, she thought moodily, making her way up to the sanctuary of her bedroom, removing the sapphire pendant as she went. What should have been a great night in her life had turned out to be a horror, all because of Leon Gregoris. She supposed she should be thankful he had left early, and she was no longer going to have to face him in London on Monday. But somehow that thought gave her no consolation.

Walking into her bedroom and closing the door behind her, she slipped out of the silver dress and, clad in only the briefest of lace briefs, dropped the pendant on the dressing table. For a moment she looked at it, her eyes narrowing; it looked vaguely familiar. Yawning widely, she dismissed the thought and, picking up her cotton nightie from the end of the bed, headed for the *en suite* bathroom. Five minutes later, her toilet complete, she slid into bed. Pulling the pink duvet up to her chin, she closed her eyes and welcomed sleep.

But it was not to be. The dark face of Leon appeared in her mind's eye; she traced her swollen lips with one finger. She could still feel his kiss, the taste of him. Nothing she did would displace his image from her brain.

Turning restlessly, she lay flat on her back and opened her eyes. She didn't want to think about the past; there were too many painful memories, and Leon's reappearance tonight had reawakened a lot of them. The trace of a smile twitched her lips. She recalled the first time her father had sent her to this very room for being naughty. That had been Leon's fault...

It had been a Saturday, just like today—or last night, she amended. Bea had been eight years of age, and her father had had visitors for the weekend: Mr Gregoris and his son. Having spent all day with adults, she'd been bored.

But at about seven o'clock in the evening she had slipped out of the gate at the bottom of the garden, something she was strictly forbidden to do. She had met two older boys from the village, Jack and Ned, and they had allowed her to play with them. Cowboys and Indians, and—wouldn't you know!—as the girl she'd got to be the Indian, captured by the cowboys, and Jack had tied her to a tree.

It had been when Ned had withdrawn a knife from his trouser pocket, saying, 'Now try some of your own medicine and see how you like it,' and grabbed her long hair prior to scalping her, that she'd begun to scream. That was how Leon had found her.

At twenty-two he'd already been a man, dressed in shorts and singlet, obviously out for his evening run. He'd pulled the two boys apart, one in each hand, shaken them and sent them sprawling on their backsides. Then he'd untied Bea and lifted the terrified little girl into his arms.

She remembered clutching him around the neck, resting her head on his chest and between sobs and hiccups telling him he was wonderful for saving her. He'd been her hero, this big, dark man with a ponytail as long as hers. At least, she'd thought so for all of ten minutes, until he'd started lecturing her on how little girls should behave. But, worse, he'd actually told her father, and she'd been sent to her room without any supper.

Looking back, Bea could see that had been the start of the love-hate relationship she shared with Leon. She had not seen a lot of him after that; his father, her dad's business partner, had been a frequent visitor, but Leon had come maybe two or three times a year, some years not even as much as that. When she had seen him he was always nice to her, though he could be a bit bossy. But then she'd thought of him as an adult friend, and most adults were bossy...

Old Mr Gregoris had died when Bea was eleven. She could remember her father going to Cyprus for the funeral, but she hadn't gone. After that Leon had come on his own to visit her father, but as often as not they'd met in London.

Then, when she'd reached her teens and begun to read the more lurid tabloids that Aunty Lil was so fond of, she'd discovered Leon was quite notorious for his lady-friends. His procession of women was well documented, and once, as a fifteen-year-old, she had teased him about it. Leon had told her not to believe everything she read in the papers. He had for once lost his sense of humour and had appeared quite upset.

Bea suddenly realised that this had been the last time Leon had visited her home until the death of her own father. Leon had appeared at his graveside on a bleak January day and held her hand. He had been a tower of strength to a very sad and frightened seventeen-year-old. Having lost his own father earlier, he'd seemed to understand exactly how she felt.

Back at the house Leon had taken charge, explaining her inheritance, insisting she complete her final year at school, and making sure Lil and Bob would look after her—though there had never been any doubt. Leon had left after a week, due to pressure of business, but had promised to return at the Easter vacation. True to his word, he had. But it had been a different Leon...

Before Bea had seen him as a sort of jocular uncle—a friend but an adult male. Then suddenly he'd begun to treat her as a grown-up. When he had arrived she had greeted him with the usual peck on the cheek, and to her amazement he had grasped her around the waist.

'Surely at nearly eighteen you can do better than that, Phoebe? I can see I'm going to have to educate you,' he'd said, and covered her lips with his own.

From then on when he'd looked at her it had been with a blatant male appreciation for a desirable female. When he'd touched her his hands had lingered just a fraction too long, and when he'd kissed her her legs had turned to jelly.

Bea shivered and pulled the duvet tightly around her. She had been such a naive young fool, and had lapped it all up.

But Leon had played his part to perfection. He was a man whose devastating charm and sophistication could make the hardest-headed businesswoman feel gauche, and he had turned the full force of his dynamic personality upon the young Bea. She'd been in awe of him.

The public success of the company since Leon had taken over was well documented. From a small import-export firm, Stephen-Gregoris had now developed into a force to be reckoned with in the world market. Leon had made them both millionaires, as he had casually pointed out on the last day of his visit...

It was a lovely spring day. A car was arriving at noon to take Leon to the airport; he would fly back to London and then on to Athens. Seated opposite him at the table in the breakfast room, Bea was feeling sad at the thought of Leon's departure; the past five days had been wonderful.

Last night he had taken her out to dinner at Twenty-One, an exclusive restaurant in Newcastle. On arriving home he had led her into the living room and pulled her down onto the couch beside him. She had snuggled up against his side with a sigh of pure contentment.

'Happy, sweetheart?' Leon had asked, and, not waiting for a reply, had turned her in his arms and kissed her. A long time later he'd raised his head and shifted slightly to look into her flushed, trusting face.

'There's something I want to ask you, Phoebe. I know...' And that had been when Lil had walked in.

'I heard you arrive so I've brought you coffee.'

Bea had not been pleased at the interruption. She'd had a sneaky suspicion that Lil was acting as a chaperone, and she'd been sure of it when the older woman had sat down and poured the coffee into three cups before asking about their evening out. An hour later Bea had gone to bed, still wondering...

Now, seated with Leon at the breakfast table, Bea sighed and drained her cup of coffee, her blue eyes resting wistfully on the top of his dark head. He was apparently oblivious to her presence, reading the morning paper. Whatever he had been going to ask her last night, he had obviously forgotten it this morning, she thought morosely. In a few hours he would be gone and it was back to studying for her, for her A level exams. A place at the University of Newcastle upon Tyne was waiting for her, providing she passed them.

'Don't look so sad. It might never happen.' Leon's deep voice cut into her morbid thoughts.

Glancing across at him, she almost said, It already has; you're leaving. But, young as she was, she had the sense to keep her true feelings to herself, and instead said, 'But it will... Exams start in six weeks' time; it's nose to the grindstone time for me. Whereas you will be flitting around the world, chatting up every beautiful woman you meet.' She tried for a teasing smile but it did not quite come off.

Her innate common sense told her Leon had simply been flirting with her the past few days. There was no way a man like him could really be interested in her on a personal level. He was kind to her because of their fathers' relationship, and because technically they were now business partners—though the reality was that Leon was her trustee, along with Mr Nicholson, her late father's lawyer, until she was twenty-one.

'Jealous, Phoebe?' he teased back, and, putting the newspaper down on the table, he stood up. 'There is no need.'

He was tall, well over six feet, and incredibly handsome; he had to be nearly thirty-two now. Far too old for her. But he looked so vitally male, so elegant in his immaculate, conservative three-piece suit, and yet subtly powerful and superbly healthy—which, given his lifestyle, was something of a miracle. If the papers were to be believed, he played as hard as he worked. Fascinated, Bea watched as he strolled around the table and reached out a hand to her.

'Come on, sweet Phoebe, a walk before I leave. And hopefully we will escape your guardian angel Lil for a while.'

Bea put her hand in his and was pulled to her feet. Five minutes later Leon, still holding her hand, opened the garden gate with his other hand, and then guided her onto the path.

They talked of her exams, her university course, her ambitions. It was only when they were out of sight of the house that Leon suddenly stopped a few feet away from a large willow tree.

'The infamous tree where you were held captive,' he declared, and grinned down at her.

Bea tilted her head back. She laughed up at him. 'Yes, and I haven't forgotten I got no supper. Because of you, I was confined to my room.'

His dark eyes narrowed for a moment on her young, girlish figure. She was wearing figure-hugging blue jeans and a blue sweatshirt. Her high, firm breasts, clearly defined against the soft fabric, made it obvious she wore no bra. Leon dropped her hand and curved an arm around her waist, pulling her against his lower torso. 'I wish I could confine you to my room.'

She looked at him, thrilled by his statement, but all her youthful uncertainty was reflected in her wide blue eyes. 'Why?' she asked.

'For heaven's sake! Don't look at me like that. You make me feel like... Never mind...' Leon hesitated, then walked on until they were at the tree. Leaning his back against the trunk, legs splayed, he turned her loosely in the circle of his arms, so she was standing between his hard-muscled thighs.

The light touch of his hands on her waist and the subtle male scent of him both conspired to make her heart leap in her chest. She wanted to move forward, just a fraction, enough to make contact with his hard body, to have that proud head bend and his firm mouth on hers. She didn't know herself. Bea had never felt like this with any man before. Only Leon had the power to turn her into a quivering heap of over-active nerves, passions, feelings...whatever! She only knew his virile masculine aura was such that it promised everything a female could desire, with the certainty that he could deliver...

'Did you ever see either of those two little monsters again?'

'What?' She jumped as his question cut into her over-heated thoughts. 'Yes, as a matter of fact I did.'

Leon sent her a mocking glance. 'Not here, I hope. Surely you weren't stupid enough to be caught twice?'

If Leon had one fault, Bea thought mutinously, it was arrogance. He was so clever, of such towering intellect, he tended to think other people were dumb.

'No, actually. Jack, the older of the two—not the one who was about to scalp me—' she clarified, 'is a good friend. He's in his second year at Oxford, and doing well, already a rugby blue. We went to a couple of parties together when he was home for the Christmas break; we have the same friends. I got a card from him last week. He's spending the Easter break in Switzerland. He's also a keen skier—in fact an all-round sportsman.' As she spoke what she had wished for earlier happened.

Leon slipped one arm completely around her waist and hauled her hard against him. With his free hand he clasped her chin and tilted her face up to his.

'Is he now?' His lips were quirking as he cast her a curious glance. 'Well, I hope he breaks a leg.'

'Leon! That's rotten.'

'No, realistic,' he returned with a laugh. 'If anyone is going to tie you up ever again, it's going to be me.' And, swinging around, it was suddenly Bea who had her back against the tree.

'You wouldn't, and anyway you have no rope,' she shot back.

'Who needs one?' Leon murmured, and, fastening her to the tree with the pressure of his large body, his dark head bent and his lips brushed softly over hers. 'Will you let me tie you to me, Phoebe?' he asked huskily, his teeth nibbling her bottom lip while his hand clasped the nape of her neck and held her head firm. He scattered kisses over her brow, her eyes, her cheekbones, and back down to her softly parted lips.

She was helpless against his gentle persuasion as he trailed kisses down her throat, and then his hand cupped her breast through the thickness of her sweater, his thumb unerringly finding its rigid tip and squeezing ever so slowly. 'Will you be tied to me, metaphorically speaking, my own sweet Phoebe? Will you be my wife?'

Of course she said yes. She said yes to everything he suggested. Their engagement would be a secret until she had finished school, and on her eighteenth birthday, in August, he would take her to the family villa in Cyprus and declare it to the world. They would marry a few weeks later and, if she liked, she could still go to university.

Bea sailed through her last term at school. Her grief at losing her father at the beginning of the year still lingered, but her love for Leon and knowing he loved her somehow made everything better. She even applied herself to her exams with a new-found vigour.

Leon telephoned every other night, wherever in the world he happened to be, and with his support and encouragement she blossomed into a confident young woman. She did have one slight argument with him in June: school was to finish in July and she wanted to join him immediately afterwards, but Leon said no. But the 'no' was tempered the next day by the arrival of a huge bouquet of red roses, and the following day came a loving letter from America, explaining the difficulties of his schedule but promising to be in England the week before her birthday—mid-August.

One morning in August Bea stood in the hall, an envelope addressed to herself in her own handwriting in her hand. 'Lil, they're here!' she yelled. Her exam results.

'Well, open it, dear,' Lil commanded, joining her. 'They won't alter for the waiting, pet.'

With trembling fingers she slit open the envelope, took one glance and then she was whirling Lil around the hall in a wild polka. 'I've passed! I've passed! Four straight As.'

To make her happiness complete, after spending two hours on the telephone calling all her friends, Leon arrived. She was still on the telephone when a deep voice murmured in her free ear, 'Miss me, Phoebe?'

Bea squeaked, 'Got to go,' and dropped the receiver on the hall table. A strong arm encircled her waist and turned her around. 'Leon, you're back,' she murmured inanely, suddenly inexplicably nervous.

Leon's hand cupped her chin and tilted her head back as his dark eyes scrutinised her lovely face. 'Is that the best you can do in the way of a welcome, Phoebe, darling?' he drawled mockingly. 'Months apart and you say "you're back"?'

'One hundred and thirty-two days, actually.' Bea glanced at her watch, 'And twenty-two hours.' Wrapping her slender arms around his neck, with a wide, beautiful smile curving her full lips, she added, 'I have missed you during every one of them.'

A long, satisfying kiss later, Bea gazed dazedly into Leon's dark eyes. 'I wasn't expecting you until tomorrow.'

'Change of plan—I have to be in Athens tomorrow.' Leon spent the next ten minutes explaining why, but Bea barely took it in. She was too entranced to have him beside her, to hear his voice, to be able to feast her eyes on his large, all-male body.

Her happy, dazed state lasted until the aeroplane touched down at Athens airport, and beyond…

Sighing, Bea let the paperback book, number one on the *New York Times* bestseller list, fall to the ground beside the sun lounger on which she was reclining. She didn't seem able to get interested in anything today.

Leon's villa was set high on the hills above Paphos, in the Greek sector of the island of Cyprus. The view before her was magnificent: an enticingly cool-looking swimming pool and beyond it the garden, flowing down the hillside in a mass of flowers and shrubs, the whole enclosed by an undulating white wall. Beyond, in the far distance, the ancient port of Paphos and its magnificent fortress stood by the Mediterranean Sea.

Her only garment was a minuscule bikini, and yet the heat was still stifling. Glancing at her half-naked body, she hauled herself into a sitting position and idly picked up a bottle of sun lotion and began massaging it into her arms and legs, across her flat stomach. The trouble was, she thought wryly, it wasn't so much the heat outside that was making her so restless, but the heat within her.

Last night had been wonderful. Leon had held a huge party and they had become officially engaged. A tiny smile pursed her lips as she twisted the magnificent dia-

mond and sapphire ring on the third finger of her left
hand. Every time she looked at it she got a lump in her
throat, not just for its beauty, but for what it represented.

Her engagement party had been perfect; she had
danced the night away in the arms of the man she loved,
the man she was going to marry, and she had met all of
Leon's friends and his stepmother, Tany, who seemed a
very nice lady. But Tany's daughter by her first marriage, Amy, Bea was not so sure about, and Amy's
friend from America, Selina, Bea had certainly not taken
to. The woman had given her the most peculiar look,
and a positively evil smile. Still, all in all it had been a
great party.

Bea sighed again, and lay back down. She only had
one slight niggle—and she knew she was being stupid—
but... After the guests had left, and the house guests had
retired for the night, finally she and Leon had been alone.
He had walked her to her bedroom door and taken her
into his arms.

Her eyes fluttered closed—just for a moment—as she
relived the sensations his kiss had aroused. Her lips had
quivered beneath the light touch of his mouth, then he
had lazily nibbled her bottom lip, his tongue exploring
when her mouth opened to him. Her hands, of their own
accord, had moved up his arms to cling to his broad
shoulders, glorying in the strength of his taut muscles
and the power of his broad frame. He'd deepened the
kiss with an ease and sensuality that had made her whole
body burn with a trembling need that reached the very
core of her being.

She'd murmured his name: 'Leon.' At last they were
engaged, and the bed was just behind the door. Her firm
young body had arched into him, the power of his arousal against her pelvis making her ache with frustration.

'No, Phoebe,' he'd murmured against her lips. 'Ten days is not too long to wait.' He'd eased her away from him. 'I want you to have a perfect wedding, and a perfect wedding night. You deserve it. And that means keeping my desire under control until then.'

Sighing for the third time, Bea rolled over onto her stomach on the lounger. It had been a noble sentiment on Leon's part, but had done nothing for the frustration burning inside her... With her head resting on her folded arms, she dozed off...

She raised her head groggily and turned onto her back, not sure what had awakened her. The lounger, placed as it was near the house, was now in the shade. 'Thank goodness for that,' she muttered to herself, realising she could have been burned to a crisp. Then she heard it again. Her name being called from inside the villa.

Good, Leon was back. He had gone into Paphos to see someone on business earlier. She was just about to stand up and make her whereabouts known when another voice floated from the open window not three yards away.

'Looking for your proposed child bride, Leon, darling?' It was Selina, the American girl, who spoke. 'I don't think you'll be in such a hurry to find her after you hear what I have to say.'

'Selina, there is nothing you have to say that I want to hear.'

'Leon, don't be like this. This is me, Selina, you're talking to. Your lover for the last three years. You can't fool me.' A shuffling sound followed.

Bea gasped and, raising her hand to her mouth, she bit hard on her knuckle to stifle her cry of pain.

'Let go, Selina, you're wasting your time. I told you it was over months ago. You career women are all the same. You say you are equal to a man in every way, and you willingly enter into an open relationship, quite clearly defined, mutual pleasure only. Then, as soon as you are told it is over, instead of acting like a man and walking away, you revert to sniffling feminine tricks.'

'Please, Leon, you have to listen to me. I know you care for me—you can't possibly love that schoolgirl. Even your stepmother said your engagement was more about cementing the business partnership firmly under your complete control than about any love on your part.'

'My reasons are my own, Selina, and are not up for discussion. Now get out of my way and stay out of it.'

'That might be hard to do. Especially in seven months' time when our child is born.'

'Impossible, and anyway I always use protection— mainly to prevent just this type of blackmail. Do yourself a favour and leave, before I have you thrown out.'

Bea could not believe her ears. This was a Leon she had never heard before: hard and totally ruthless. But worse was to follow.

'Aren't you forgetting something, Leon? Two months ago, at the Mackenzies' house party in Newport? You flew in, partied half the night, and woke up in the morning in my bed. Protection was not something you bothered about. I know; I was there...'

For a long moment there was silence. Then, 'You bitch, Selina. You did it deliberately. Didn't you?'

Bea didn't hear the rest of the conversation. She had heard enough. Staggering to her feet, she silently crept around the outside of the house and entered by the kitchen. She took the servants' stairs to her room and once inside locked the door. She collapsed on the bed, but could not cry. She was too traumatised for tears. Instead she stared blankly at the white walls, asking herself over and over again, How could I have been such a fool?

CHAPTER THREE

BEA had been used, exploited by the first man she had ever let near her. Before Leon she had dated a few boys of her own age, and exchanged the odd fumbled kiss, but nothing like the passionate interludes Leon had introduced her to. She should have realised a sophisticated, sexually mature man like Leon couldn't possibly be interested in a naive young girl such as herself unless he had an ulterior motive. But she had blindly agreed with everything Leon had said. She'd even put up with him calling her Phoebe, when she much preferred Bea...

Nausea clawed at her stomach; the sense of betrayal ate into her very being. That she could be so wrong about a man she had known almost all her life, a man she would have trusted *with* her life, made her burn with shame at her own gullibility.

She thumped the bed with her clenched fists and shouted out loud, 'Fool, fool, fool!' Then the tears came. Bea cried until she had no tears left, and her throat was raw and dry. Finally she slowly sat up. She had no idea how long she had been in the bedroom, but it was already getting dark. Confirmation, if she needed any more, of how little Leon actually thought of her.

On his return to the villa, his eager calling of her name had roused her from sleep. But since his conversation with Selina he certainly hadn't bothered trying to find Bea again.

She heaved herself off the bed and walked into the bathroom. One look in the mirror, and if she could have cried again she would have. Red-rimmed, swollen eyes stared out of a face as white as a ghost's. She had no idea how she was going to face Leon ever again.

Stripping off her bikini, she stepped into the shower and turned on the cold water. She stood beneath the freezing spray, praying it would numb her body and brain, but it was no good. The image of Leon and Selina together tortured her mind. Three years... They had been lovers for three years, and they were having a baby together. She heard again Leon's furious outburst: 'You did it deliberately.' And that was what hurt most of all.

Leon hadn't tried to deny the child was his. He was simply furious at being caught by the oldest trick in the book. Bea stepped out of the shower, wrapped a towel around herself and walked back into the bedroom. She stopped by the dressing table, pulled the diamond ring off her finger and dropped it on the polished surface. Her engagement ring. What a joke! While she had considered herself engaged since Easter, when Leon had asked her to marry him and she had said yes, he had obviously felt no such commitment. He had continued sleeping with his long-time lover.

It was not so surprising, really, she thought as mechanically she set about getting dressed. She had always known Leon was the Lothario type, but in her youthful naivety she had let herself believe she was the one person who could change him. A hollow laugh escaped her. She remembered last night and their impassioned kisses, and then his denial of what she had quite obviously been offering, his high moral stance. He wanted her to have the perfect wedding, and wedding night. What a lie!

Sadly Bea realised he probably didn't even want her in a sexual way. No, what he wanted was control of her share of the company. With that thought her sorrow began to change, and by the time she was standing in front of the mirror once more, about to put on her make-up, she wasn't sad but mad... Mad with a cold fury. Then it came to her—a way to escape with her pride intact and without revealing what she knew.

In the end it was simple. Bea walked into the dining room, not a scrap of make-up on her pale face, her long hair tied up in a childish ponytail and wearing the simple blue and white candy-striped dress she had included in her luggage, thinking it would come in useful if she were messing around. She knew she looked ridiculously young, but that was the idea.

Tany, Leon's stepmother, Amy and Selina were elegantly gowned and already seated at the table. But Leon was standing near the door and crossed straight to Bea's side. He bent his head to kiss her. She saw it coming and deliberately moved so that his lips brushed her cheek and not her mouth.

'Something the matter, Phoebe?' he asked solicitously.

Bea almost snapped back, Yes, you, you snake! But, biting her tongue, she simply turned her face up to his, giving him the full benefit of her red, swollen eyes. 'Not exactly.'

'Please sit down, you two. We want to eat,' Tany commanded.

Leon cast Bea a worried glance, but held out a chair for her and then slid into the one next to her.

It was Tany who noticed first. 'Bea, where is your ring, child? You don't want to lose it. Knowing Leon, it will have cost a fortune. And what has happened to your eyes?'

Dramatically Bea pushed back her chair and jumped to her feet, acting for all she was worth. The last thing she felt like doing was sharing a dinner with this group.

'Please, you will have to excuse me. I'm not hungry.' Glancing down at Leon's upturned face, surprise and puzzlement evident in his expression, she added, 'I really am terribly sorry but it has all been a mistake. I realised this afternoon. It is beautiful here, but I—I am h-homesick.' She deliberately stuttered. 'I miss my friends and Lil, and the cool English summer, and I don't want to get married, not yet.'

A solitary tear rolled down her cheek, lending credit to her story, but in actual fact it was a tear of self-pity, an emotion she despised. Brushing her cheek with the back of her hand, she saw Leon's dark eyes narrow assessingly on her pale face. Then slowly he got to his feet, and tried to put an arm around her shoulders.

'Don't be silly, Phoebe. It's probably just bridal nerves.' He smiled. 'I promise everything will be fine.'

Patronising swine, she thought, and, twisting out from under his arm, she turned to face him.

'It will not be all right because I do not want to marry you. I want to go home and get on with my studies, my life. I'm sorry. I think it was because of my father dying so recently. I needed a father figure, and so I latched onto you. But that is no reason to get married.'

It took every ounce of nerve and self-control Bea possessed to hold Leon's now angry gaze and deliver her final comment. 'I realise now I'm not ready for marriage or commitment. I'm only just eighteen, far too young, and you…well, you're…' She trailed off, not so subtly implying that Leon was too old for her.

It had been the reference to age that had clinched it, Bea mused, safely ensconced on the aeroplane back to England the next day. In her mind's eye she could still see the look of frustrated fury on his darkly handsome face as Selina and Amy had had the temerity to laugh.

True, he had made another attempt to change her mind much later. He had walked into her bedroom and tried, with his sexual expertise, to kiss her into submission.

But knowing his lover Selina was downstairs had given Bea the strength to remain cold in his arms. How long she could have continued doing so was anybody's guess. Because she'd still wanted him, even as she'd hated herself for feeling that way. But the arrival of Tany to check that Bea was all right had stopped Leon cold. And, in Tany's presence, Bea had given him back his ring.

Yawning widely, Bea turned over and curled up into a foetal position. She yawned again. Tomorrow was the first day of the rest of her life. The past was past. Leon was no threat to her peace of mind any more, she told herself groggily. As for her reaction to his kiss earlier, it was simply because she had drunk too much champagne and he had caught her off guard. It would never happen again. Only a fool made the same mistake twice, and at twenty-one, with a degree in her pocket, Bea was nobody's fool...

The drive down to London was not as bad as Bea had expected. The Sunday traffic was light, and she arrived at the underground car park of the mansion block that housed her late father's apartment at five in the evening. It was a simple matter to transfer her two suitcases to the lift, and moments later she was plonking them on the bed in the only bedroom.

Her father had originally had his office in Newcastle, but after the death of Nick Gregoris, and Leon taking the place of his father, the firm had expanded rapidly. The English headquarters had been moved to London, at Leon's instigation. Bea had been twelve when her father had begun travelling to London on a Monday and staying two or three days, safe in the knowledge that Bea was at school all day and Lil was there to look after her.

Glancing around the familiar bedroom, Bea thought

fondly of the times in the school holidays when her dad had taken her to London with him occasionally. With a shake of her fair head, she told herself not to get sentimental, and set about unpacking her belongings.

Ten minutes later she stared in amazement at the kitchen table. Someone had anticipated her arrival. A huge vase full of red roses was at the centre, and propped against it was an envelope. Picking it up, she quickly slit it open and withdrew a sheet of notepaper. She recognised the bold, sloping writing immediately. It was from Leon—a rather childish poem.

> *Enjoy the roses while you may*
> *Tomorrow is a working day.*
> *The fridge is stocked, the larder too*
> *Behave yourself until I'm with you.*

A small smile twitched her full lips; she had forgotten. Almost every time she had seen Leon when she was a child he had made up a stupid rhyme for her. She racked her brain, trying to remember the first one.

> *The lovely lady fair*
> *Almost lost her hair*
> *By playing near a willow*
> *When she should have been asleep on her pillow*

Bea's grin broadened. Leon had been good fun as an uncle figure. Pity their relationship had not stayed that way. The smile faded from her face to be replaced with a frown.

What did he mean, *until I'm with you*? The note fell unnoticed from her hand and quickly she turned around. Bea opened the refrigerator door and was not surprised to see it stocked full, including a bottle of white wine.

The cupboard was the same. Uneasily she walked into the living room and glanced around. Had Leon been here? And, more importantly, how the hell had he got in? She had the only key. Anyway, he was supposed to be in America.

Suddenly the safety of her apartment seemed threatened, and she didn't like it, not one bit... Think, woman, think, she told herself. Of course! A sigh of relief escaped her and she sank down on the sofa. The caretaker had a master key. Leon must have sent the note and instructions to provide the goodies to the caretaker.

Relieved to have the mystery settled, she made full use of the food provided to make herself an omelette and salad, washed down with a glass of wine, then she went to bed.

'Ready to go yet, Bea?'

Bea glanced up and smiled at the tall red-headed girl asking the question. Actually, Margot was a woman in every sense of the word, about thirty-eight years old. As personal assistant to Tom Jordan, she knew everything about the business.

'I thought, if you have nothing special to do tonight, we could stop off for a pizza and a glass of wine or two on the way home.'

'Oh, sorry, Margot, I forgot to mention—I've arranged to meet a boyfriend for dinner and I'm going straight from here.'

'Ah, a heavy date with the male of the species—and you with only two weeks of living in the city. How do you do it?'

Bea grinned. 'His name is Jack, I've known him for years, and he comes from my home town.'

'Interesting, is he?' Margot queried, with a suggestive flicker of her eyebrows.

'Well, he did once tie me up.'

'Bondage... This I must hear. If you get back before eleven pop in and tell me all about him. It's about the only way I get a thrill nowadays. Vicariously.'

'Liar,' Bea chuckled. 'I've heard you on the telephone to a certain financial advisor in the office three floors above us.'

Margot winked. 'Enough said. Tom left half an hour ago, so I'm off. Enjoy yourself.' And, closing the door behind her as she left, Bea heard her shout, 'Don't forget to lock the outer door.'

A lingering smile played around Bea's lips. She could still hear a mumble coming from next door—probably Margot talking to herself. She was prone to speaking her thoughts out loud.

Though Bea hated to admit that Leon could be right about anything, he had been right about Margot becoming a friend. Over the past two weeks the two women had developed a good working relationship, and had also become firm pals.

The offices of Stephen-Gregoris occupied the first floor of a prestigious block in the heart of the city, and, arriving for work on her first day, Bea had naturally felt nervous. A rather superior blonde girl had shown her to what was to be her office, but in fact was a small partitioned section of Margot's much larger one, which in turn led straight to the manager's. Then Margot had walked out of Tom Jordan's office, apologised for not being there to greet her, and had immediately taken Bea under her wing.

Only Tom Jordan and Margot knew Bea owned part of the company, but Margot showed no resentment at the fact. She had taken Bea on a tour of the office, and introduced her to all the staff with the explanation that Bea was the new graduate trainee who was to work in each department for a few weeks to get the feel of the operation and would probably end up in the finance section.

The fact that Margot's apartment was in the same block as Bea's was an added bonus. They'd quickly decided to travel to work together, and had shared the occasional meal or a gossip over coffee.

Stretching, Bea glanced at her watch: it was after six. She was meeting Jack at Covent Garden, a short taxi ride away. Jack had done extremely well for himself; he'd gained a first at Oxford and for the past two years had held a high-profile job with a top merchant bank in London. It would be good fun to catch up on all his news.

With a contented sigh at the completion of the last spreadsheet, Bea switched off her computer terminal and stood up. It was very quiet, but then the building usually emptied early on a Friday.

Bea reckoned she had just enough time for a wash and brush-up, and, with a quick glance around the room, she picked up her bag from the desk, checked she had the office key, and left.

Crossing Margot's office, Bea hesitated. What was that sound she'd heard? She turned and looked around. That's funny, she thought, the door to Tom Jordan's office is half open. It's unlike Margot to forget to lock it.

She waited a moment longer, but everything was quiet, and so, with a shrug of her shoulders, she crossed to where she knew Margot kept a spare key in her desk drawer. And got another surprise. The key was not in the drawer, but lying on the desktop. The woman's mind was slipping; Bea would tease her about it tomorrow.

A couple of seconds later and Bea had closed and locked Tom's door, and the outer one behind her.

Singing softly to herself—she was looking forward to

tonight—Bea headed for the ladies' room. Stephen-Gregoris provided excellent facilities for the female staff. A pleasant restroom with a locker provided for everyone, two shower cubicles and the usual accompaniments. Opening her locker, she withdrew a towel and toilet bag and crossed to the row of vanity basins occupying one wall.

She was not going to change; the smart blue suit, with its double-breasted short-sleeved jacket and short straight skirt, which she had worn all day with a high-necked white blouse, would do for the evening—minus the blouse. Bea removed her jacket and the blouse and hung them on the back of a chair, and then quickly washed and redid her make-up. Slipping the jacket back on, she fastened the buttons and checked her image in the mirror.

She pursed her lips; the deep vee of the jacket lapels maybe revealed a little too much cleavage. She would have to remember not to bend forward and reveal the lace of her bra—or maybe she could remove the bra! What the hell? she told herself. You're in the city now… And she did. Then, rashly, she unpinned her hair from its rather severe chignon and let it fall loose about her shoulders.

Her jacket back in place, she stopped in the act of picking up her hairbrush. Was that someone hurrying down the corridor? Must be Security… Tipping her head forward, she brushed her hair until it crackled with life and then swung it back. The effect was rather good, even if she did say so herself. Having been pinned up all day, her usually straight silver-blonde hair had developed a rather nice bouncy curl around the ends.

A quick spray of her favourite perfume, and she was ready. Quickly she replaced her toiletries in the locker, with her discarded bra and blouse, and with a last look at her reflection she made for the door.

Bea stepped out into the hall. Just at that moment the office door she had so recently locked was flung open. She expected to see a security man, but what she actually saw stopped her in her tracks.

'You—you crazy little bitch. I might have guessed,' Leon Gregoris roared, and came barrelling towards her, a security man hard on his heels, apologising madly.

'Leave it—and us. I will deal with this,' Leon snarled at the poor man, and Bea watched in open-mouthed amazement as the security man disappeared at a run. She turned back just in time to have Leon grab her by the arm. 'I suppose you thought that was funny—a stupid, childish practical joke. My God! Are you never going to grow up?'

Bea shook her head. It was a dream—it had to be. One minute she was in an empty office building, preparing for a date, the next Leon had appeared out of nowhere, breathing fire and brimstone. She hadn't been far wrong when she'd thought he looked like a warlock. She glanced curiously up into his red, furious face; the devil himself might be nearer the mark.

'Well, woman, what have you to say for yourself?'

'I haven't the foggiest notion what you're talking about,' she offered, with another shake of her head. He was dressed in a dark blue suit and white silk shirt, with a maroon silk tie half undone around his neck. The white of his shirt only served to emphasise his darkly flushed features. 'Where did you come from?' she asked in obvious puzzlement.

Hell itself, if the flames leaping in his black eyes were anything to go by as they seared down into hers!

'Don't give me that wide-eyed innocent look. You deliberately locked me in that office. Didn't you?'

Suddenly she was aware of the fierce grip of his hand around her forearm; the heat of his large body seemed to reach out to engulf her. Swallowing hard, she tried to pull free. 'Locked you in the office?' she muttered inanely. 'I don't know what you're talking about. I didn't even know you were here,' she added, gathering her composure. 'I think you've had a brainstorm. Maybe you should see a doctor.'

'I sometimes wonder that myself. Why I put up with you I will never know,' Leon grated, scowling down at her. 'You drive me to distraction almost every time we meet. What is it with you? Is it your purpose in life to deliberately make me look a fool?'

'I don't have to; you do that very well yourself. That poor security man looked petrified. What on earth did you say to him?' She watched him warily; she saw him take a few deep breaths, his massive chest expand and contract beneath the soft fabric of his shirt. For a second he closed his eyes, and then he opened them again.

'Margot didn't tell you I had arrived, did she?'

'No, she left half an hour ago.'

'Oh, damn! And you, like the conscientious worker you are, locked all the doors before leaving?'

'Of course.' Bea wished he would just let go of her; now he had calmed down she recognised a much more disturbing glitter in his dark eyes.

'Sorry, sweetheart, it was my mistake.' And before she could say a word he hauled her into his arms and his mouth swooped down over hers.

She was too stunned to move. And after the first touch of his lips, so soft, so gentle, she found she didn't want to. He coaxed a response from her that she was helpless to deny.

A long moment later Leon lifted his head and stared

down into her flushed, bemused face. 'That is how I meant to greet you.'

An angry Leon she could deal with, but when he was being charming it was another matter altogether. Shoving her hand between their two bodies, she tried to ease away. 'I preferred you angry,' she breathed heavily, fighting down the urge to sink back against him. 'But I would like an explanation.'

A wry grin twisted his lips. 'I owe you that much, I suppose. I arrived at Heathrow almost three hours ago, and have been stuck in the Friday rush-hour traffic for most of the time since then. I intended going straight to my hotel and then calling you, but the office was nearer and, basically, I was desperate to use the bathroom. I dashed in as Margot was leaving. She opened Jordan's door for me and left the key on the desk for me to close it.'

Bea could feel the beginnings of a chuckle starting deep in her chest. It was ridiculous, she knew, but the idea of the great Leon Gregoris being caught short like any other human being was highly amusing. 'I thought I heard mumbling but presumed it was Margot talking to herself,' she offered quickly, in an effort to control her real desire to laugh.

'That would have been me,' Leon said quite seriously. 'I had no idea you were still here. So you can imagine my surprise when I tried to leave and found myself locked in. For a horrible moment I had a vision of spending the weekend in the office, until I remembered Security. I rang them and it did nothing for my temper when it took them over fifteen minutes to answer. Then, when I was finally free and saw you standing in the corridor, I jumped to the conclusion it was a practical joke on your part, and saw red.'

He had looked a bit like a charging bull, Bea thought

on reflection, and she could restrain herself no longer. 'The great Leon locked in the loo,' she spluttered, and burst out laughing.

'It wasn't funny.' His hands tightened on her arms. Glancing up at him, her blue eyes dancing with amusement, she saw his lips twitch, then break into a smile and finally into outright laughter.

The shared humour seemed to clear the air between them, and Bea, still smiling, glanced at the watch on her wrist as she pushed her hand against his chest again. 'It is good to see you, Leon, and I'm glad we can still share a joke, but would you mind letting me go? I have a date.' She felt the brief flicker of tension in him, and suddenly she was free.

He stepped back and really looked at her, his dark eyes skimming over the silver hair in tumbled disarray, the plunging neckline of her jacket and the short skirt, moving down her long legs and back to her face. 'He is a lucky man; you look ready for it,' he drawled mockingly.

So much for the brief moment of accord, Bea thought dryly. Leon just couldn't help himself. If it had been any other man who had said that to her, she would probably have slapped his face. But she had more sense than to try it with Leon. 'And you with your vast experience would know, of course,' she shot back, and, turning, walked away.

He caught up with her at the elevator. 'As I am the cause of your delay I insist on giving you a lift.'

'No, thank you.'

'Be reasonable, Phoebe; you'll never get a taxi in the rush hour, and in any case I feel it is my duty to check the man out.'

Bea's gasp of outrage was cut short by his hand at her

back urging her into the elevator. 'Now wait a minute, you pompous...'

'You don't have a minute; you're already late.' Leon grinned, and pushed the button for the foyer.

He was doing it again, taking control as though she were still a child. The trip to the ground floor was too quick for her to state her case. Before she knew it she was out on the pavement, with Leon's arm at her elbow leading her towards a low-slung black sports car. Parked on a double yellow line, and of course he hadn't got a ticket, Bea thought blackly, eyeing the traffic warden standing not two feet away. The swine had no doubt conned her as well.

'All right, Mr Gregoris, but don't make a habit of it,' the woman simpered, and was treated to one of Leon's megawatt smiles.

'Thank you, Officer. I won't, I promise.'

Like all his promises: easily given but with no substance, Bea thought with a sad shake of her head. Leon would never change...

CHAPTER FOUR

SEATED in the passenger seat of Leon's car, Bea cast her companion a baleful look. 'I wanted to get a taxi; this is totally unnecessary,' she said flatly.

She might as well have talked to a brick wall. Leon took not the blindest bit of notice, but simply stared straight ahead as he manoeuvred the powerful car through the busy city streets. He really was impossible, Bea thought for the thousandth time. Why she bothered trying to argue with him she did not know. For the rest of the short journey she ignored him.

'Where are we meeting this guy?'

'You are not meeting him, I am.' She instructed Leon to go to Covent Garden. Unfastening her seat belt on arriving, Bea opened the door and jumped out of the car. 'Thanks for the lift,' she cried jauntily, and, swinging on her heel, she set off down the road. Ten seconds later a large arm fell across her shoulders.

'No, Phoebe, my sweet. *We* are.'

Angrily she shrugged one shoulder, trying to shake Leon off. 'Will you let go of me? And don't call me Phoebe,' she flashed back.

'No to both, and a word of warning...'

'You—warn me? It should be the other way around. Women should be warned about you, you...you...over-sexed lech,' she spluttered in exasperation. The taste of him still lingered on her lips from that kiss in the office. If only he would take his arm from her shoulder, she would feel a lot safer. She shrugged again. Being held by Leon had a disastrous effect on her senses, sending

51

her pulse rate into overdrive however much she tried to control it.

'Please yourself. But if I were you I wouldn't shrug quite so energetically—unless you want the world to see you're not wearing a bra. Not that I mind; from my position the view is magnificent,' he opined, amusement lurking in his tone.

Colour flooded up her throat and over her face. A quick glance at her neckline and then up at Leon, and she realised that from his superior height he was staring straight down her cleavage. 'You're a pervert!' she spat. But if she thought that would dent his supreme confidence she was wrong!

'Sorry to disappoint, Phoebe, but I like my women beautiful and my sex straight.' He squeezed her shoulder. 'But for you I'll get kinky, if you want me to.' And he laughed out loud at her furious face.

She felt like stamping her feet with rage and embarrassment but, by a terrific effort of will, she controlled herself enough to stare boldly up into his amused eyes and say cuttingly, 'I don't want you, kinky or otherwise, and I wish you would go now.' For a second she saw a flash of something like hurt in his black eyes, but decided she had been imagining it two seconds later.

'Foolish Phoebe, you should never challenge a man like that.' Sweeping her up in his arms, he kissed her long and hard.

At first Bea could not believe it was happening again. But, standing in the middle of the pavement, locked against his hard body and with his mouth covering hers, she was too shocked to resist and then it was too late… Her traitorous body arched against him, and when his tongue plunged into her mouth she was lost.

A group of young men jostling them and shouting, 'Way to go!' finally broke them apart.

Bea, chest heaving, eyes blazing, glared up at Leon. He smiled—he actually smiled back at her. 'Are you mad? It's still daylight,' she cried rather inanely. As if it made any difference *when* he grabbed her, she silently fumed. He had to stop...

'No, just proving a point. Now come on, Phoebe.' Leon looked around over the top of her head. 'Where are we meeting this bloke?'

Her heart was still pounding from his kiss, and her legs were none too steady, so she gave up. It was a waste of time trying to defy Leon. When he made up his mind about something it was impossible to shake him off.

'Follow me,' she muttered, striding along the pavement. 'Here it is,' she said with an angry glance at Leon.

'It's certainly not the Ritz.' He grimaced and, opening the door, stepped back to allow her to enter.

The Muck and Money was obviously not a place Leon would choose to frequent. Served him right; he wasn't invited, Bea thought with a smug smile as she walked past him into the bar and looked around.

'Bea! Over here.' A tall, blond, strikingly handsome young man, smartly dressed in a grey Armani suit, pushed his way through the crowd.

Bea grinned up into his sparkling blue eyes, delighted to see him. 'Jack, trust you to find the liveliest place in town. What happened to the quiet drink?' she prompted, laughing. It was good to see him; he reminded her of home.

Planting a swift kiss on her lips, he replied, 'And it's great to see you too, Bea. Come and meet the gang.' He reached out his hand towards her.

Leon chose that moment to intervene. Stepping forward, he effectively blocked Jack from taking Bea's hand. His black eyes narrowed and shuttered, he studied the younger man. 'Introduce me to your friend, Phoebe,' he demanded hardily, not asking but ordering.

Bea looked from Jack to Leon. They were both tall, both incredibly handsome, but where Jack's face was open and laughing Leon's expression was one of bland social correctness. Her eyes clashed with his and she felt an inexplicable little shiver race through her. His tall, wide-shouldered presence exuded an aura of perfectly controlled powerful masculinity, and yet she sensed something in his stance, a threat of aggression barely held in check.

'Phoebe.' His lips tightened, as if her silence angered him, and quickly she burst into speech.

'Leon—my old friend Jack,' she said, and, turning to smile at the younger man, she added, 'Jack, dear, my boss, Leon.'

'How do you do, sir?' Jack held out his hand, the epitome of politeness.

'Pleased to meet you, but Leon will do,' Leon said curtly, looking anything but pleased.

'Why, thank you, sir...I mean Leon,' amended Jack, disconcerted by the obvious hostility emanating from the other man. 'Would you like to join us for a drink, sir...Leon?'

Bea, listening to the exchange, had to stifle a giggle. Leon did not like the 'sir' one jot. It put him firmly in a different generation. Suddenly she saw a chance to get her own back on the arrogant devil. She quickly intervened before Leon could answer.

'Leon kindly offered to give me a lift because I was running late, but this is not really his scene.' She raised cool blue eyes to clash with angry black. 'Thank you for the lift, Leon,' she drawled with thinly veiled sarcasm. 'But I know you're a very busy man. Please don't let us delay you any longer.' And, moving slightly, she slid her arm under Jack's, leaning in towards him.

For a moment she thought she had goaded Leon too far, when she saw his handsome features darken with fury, but, amazingly, he simply forced a smile to his hard mouth, and only Bea recognised that it did not reach his eyes.

'You're right of course, Phoebe. I am rather tied up at...' Then he quite deliberately hesitated. 'Tied up,' he repeated, and, turning the full force of his powerful gaze on the hapless Jack, he exclaimed loudly in mock surprise, 'I thought I'd met you before! You're the guy who likes tying up young girls.'

In the immediate vicinity there was a sudden hush, and as Bea watched poor Jack went red to the roots of his hair with puzzled embarrassment. 'Leon...' she said furiously, about to give him a piece of her mind, but Jack found his voice.

'Oh, that was you! I remember now. But we were just fooling around... It was a game...' Jack was making it worse with every word. 'It was a long time ago, sir.'

'Well, I trust you have grown out of the habit. Phoebe is a very close friend of mine and under my protection.' And, with a malicious grin at Bea's thunderous face, Leon added smoothly, 'Why, she was only remarking on the way here that she is not into kinky sex.'

The swine had done it again, Bea raged. Every time she tried to outwit Leon, he always got the last word. She felt like kicking him, and actually lifted her foot, she was so mad. He had quite deliberately embarrassed both Jack and herself. But, before she could give free rein to her anger, Leon stepped back, grinning, as if he knew what she had intended.

'Don't forget I'm picking you up for dinner at seven tomorrow night, Phoebe,' he said, and with a casual wave of his hand he added mockingly, 'Enjoy yourself, kids.' Then he was gone.

'Phew! Bea, are you sure you're just working for that man? I got the distinct impression he considers you his property,' said Jack, urging her through the press of bodies to a corner table where five people were already seated. 'And fancy him remembering that stupid childish game. He must have a memory like an elephant.'

'Right at this moment I wish a herd of elephants would trample the damn man into the ground,' Bea said feelingly. Where did Leon get off, telling her he was taking her out tomorrow night? 'In his dreams,' she muttered under her breath.

'Hey, lighten up, old girl. We're here to have fun.' And have fun they did... Much to Bea's surprise, after the disastrous start to the evening. A few more bottles of wine and a lot of laughter later, they all piled into two taxis and headed for some new restaurant Jack had heard of.

They fell from the cabs in a laughing bunch, a short walk from the entrance to the restaurant, but as they strolled towards the door all the amusement left Bea's flushed face.

On the point of leaving the premises, with the doormen in obeisance, was Leon Gregoris, elegantly dressed in a dinner suit, and not alone. Clinging to his arm was a model, as famous for her lovers as she was for her modelling career.

Bea slipped behind the group, hoping Leon would not see her. But she need not have worried; his whole attention was on the gorgeous woman as he ushered her into the passenger seat of a waiting car with a lingering kiss on her lips, before walking around and slipping into the driving seat.

Bea stared at the departing car, a sick feeling in the

pit of her stomach. It wasn't the wine she had drunk; she had been careful. hIt was the shock of actually seeing Leon kiss another woman. She watched until the car was out of sight, unaware of her surroundings.

Leon, her friend for most of her life. She had rationalised their brief engagement by looking upon him as the man who had done her a favour by introducing her to the sensual side of her nature as a teenager, without compromising her virginity. But the man who had kissed her in the street a few short hours ago really *was* a womaniser. Staring at the empty road, suddenly she felt icy cold although it was a warm night. It was one thing to think someone was a womaniser, but it was quite another to see it with one's own eyes, she thought sadly.

And in that moment she really grew up. She finally accepted that Leon was a good laugh, a good friend, but beyond redemption where women were concerned. A woman would have to be an absolute idiot to love the man. With a sigh and shake of her blonde head for something lost for ever, she swiftly joined her friends, who were discussing where to go next.

Obviously they were not going to get into the restaurant, she deduced from the conversation. But then none of them had the clout of Leon Gregoris, she thought wryly.

Leon! Odd, but in all the time she had known him she had never actually seen him with a woman. Oh, she had read the newspapers, knew his reputation. But she had never actually seen him in the flesh, so to speak, with another woman. Even in Cyprus, when she had discovered his betrayal, Bea had heard him with Selina but she had not seen him so much as touch the woman in her presence. Just imagining them together had been bad enough at the time.

Bea straightened her shoulders and looked around.

Seeing Leon with his model was the best thing that could have happened to her, she realised honestly. She had always known he was a rake, and any lingering romantic illusions left over from her teenage years were finally put to rest now. Leon had taught her a valuable lesson. Love and sex were not the same thing. From now on she was going to enjoy life and go for what she wanted, with no regrets.

'Andy,' she called to a rather attractive young man of Italian extraction who was one of their party. She had apparently been paired off with him. 'Where are we going next? I feel like dancing.'

Bea groaned and rolled over on the bed. A thousand little gnomes were playing a xylophone in her head.

No, it was not a xylophone; the gnomes were ringing bells. Campanal—Campanol— What did one call bell-ringers? It had gone—along with half her brain, she thought groggily.

So, this was what one called a hangover! She tried to think clearly. She remembered drinking and dancing half the night away at a top nightclub. How had she got home? That was right—it was coming back to her now: that nice Andy had brought her home in a taxi.

'Oh, my Lord, my head—my stomach,' Bea groaned. Never again—her first and last hangover, she vowed. But why did the gnomes keep ringing? No, not gnomes! The telephone!

Reaching out her hand, she felt around the bedside table and knocked the receiver off; she groped a bit more and finally her hand closed around it. Slowly she lifted the receiver, and even more slowly forced her reluctant eyes to open. She blinked in the harsh glare of sunlight filling the room. But, thank goodness, the ringing had stopped. Faintly she could hear a voice calling.

'Phoebe.'

Dragging herself half up the bed, she rested on one elbow. 'Yes,' was all she could get out.

'So you are there. I was beginning to wonder if you had stayed out all night.' Leon's deep voice vibrated in her ear.

She had not, but he probably had, she thought with sudden clarity, remembering the sultry seductress. 'What do you want, Leon?' she asked.

'That is a leading question, my sweet Phoebe,' Leon's mocking voice drawled suggestively. 'I never had you pegged as a woman who liked dirty talk on the telephone. But you know me, always one to oblige. So tell me, are you naked? I can see your long pale hair tumbled around your firm breasts—'

'Put a sock in it, Leon,' she cut in. 'I know you too well.' She was in no mood for his brand of teasing innuendo this morning. In fact, she realised, hauling herself into a sitting position, the sound of his voice, which usually brought her out in goosebumps, had absolutely no effect now.

'You mean you think you do,' he said, with an edge of cynicism. 'But down to business. I'll be a bit late tonight—something has come up.' Bea just bet it had, in the form of a luscious model, but she said nothing, simply listened. 'So I'll pick you up at seven-thirty.'

'Leon, I do not want to have dinner with you. We are partners in business, and anything you wish to discuss with me can be done in the office in working hours, nine to five, Monday to Friday.' She was quite proud of her response, given that her head was splitting. Maybe seeing him with one of his women and getting drunk had cured her of her stupid reaction to Leon. Amazingly she was no longer intimidated by the man. But equally she had no desire to go out with him.

'Nine to five? Nice if you can get it,' Leon drawled mockingly. 'Fortunately for the profitability of the company, *I* work seven days a week. Be ready and waiting. I don't want to have to come looking for you,' he concluded, an edge of steel in his tone.

Wincing, Bea pushed a hand through her tangled hair, her eyes half closed against the light. 'Okay, okay,' she reluctantly agreed. She hadn't the strength to argue, and actually she no longer cared much one way or the other. 'Bye,' she said, ending the conversation and dropping the receiver back on the rest.

Gingerly she moved her legs over the edge of the bed and sat for a moment, fighting down a wave of dizziness. Bad—but not too bad! Bea slowly got to her feet. Once in the shower with a refreshing stream of water massaging her flesh she was well on her way to recovery. By the time she was dressed in jeans and tee-shirt, with a cup of coffee in her hand, Bea was congratulating herself on having solved the problem of Leon.

Curled up on the sofa, sipping her coffee, she reached a conclusion: the events of last night had acted as a catharsis. Finally she could see Leon clearly for who and what he was, without the baggage of her teenager emotions and ideas to blur the picture. As for going out to dinner with him, no problem; they would discuss work and part friends...

She was still of the same opinion several hours later when the doorbell rang. She crossed to open the front door, pausing to glance at her reflection in the hall mirror. She was dressed in a simple halter-neck sheath dress, navy-trimmed, in cream—plain but sophisticated, she hoped. On her feet she wore three-inch-high stiletto-heeled strappy navy sandals.

She had taken care with her make-up, adding a grey eyeliner and a little extra eyeshadow to accentuate her wide blue eyes, a touch of brown-black mascara to her long lashes and a subtle dark pink lipgloss on her full lips. She was ready...

The bell rang again. 'Impatient pig,' she muttered, opening the door.

'I heard that, Phoebe!' Leon, looking dark, dangerous and incredibly attractive in a formal black dinner suit, stared down at her, a cynical smile twisting his firm lips. 'Gracious as ever, I see.'

Inexplicably Bea felt the colour rise in her face. 'Sorry,' she mumbled, and immediately wanted to take the apology back. It did not fit in with her new-found determination to deal with Leon on a mature level.

It was not a very auspicious start to the evening. But surprisingly, a couple of hours later, seated opposite Leon at a table set with the finest linen and crystal in a small, exclusive French restaurant, Bea felt totally relaxed.

Leon had been a model of decorum all evening. He had asked her how she was settling in at the London office, and asked her opinion on the staff, and how the place was run. More importantly he had listened to her views. They'd chatted about all aspects of the business, worldwide, and, Bea thought, for the first time ever Leon was actually treating her as an intelligent adult.

If now and then her eyes lingered too long on his sensuous mouth, or the soft fall of his black hair over his brow, or his long-fingered, expressive hands as he made a point, Bea had no trouble squashing her body's response to his potent masculinity. She simply conjured in her mind's eye the image of Leon last night.

Ironically, he had been leaving the same restaurant where they were seated tonight; maybe he had sat at the same table, and he had probably been wearing the same dinner suit. Bea recalled him kissing his glamorous model as he'd ushered her into his car...

She briefly looked around the dimly lit restaurant, noting the covert glances directed at Leon from almost every woman present. In a way, Bea didn't blame him. He was an exceptionally attractive, virile male, and wealthy with it. Why shouldn't he take advantage of what was obviously on offer? It wasn't up to her to pass judgement on his lifestyle.

Bea replaced her spoon on her plate and sighed. The meal had been perfect: smoked salmon pâté followed by Supreme de Volaille Alexandra—poached chicken breast with cheese sauce and asparagus, with slices of truffle added. And for their sweet there had been a delicious summer pudding.

'That was delicious. I'm absolutely stuffed full.'

'Stuffed, hmm?' Leon repeated smoothly, his expression remarkably bland. Bea glanced at him and caught the glint of wicked amusement in his dark eyes. His lips tilted at the corners in a brief, very masculine grin before he added, 'I could comment, but I won't.'

Mellow with fine food and fine wine, Bea grinned back. 'You're an impossible man, Leon,' she said, with a rueful shake of her head. How was it that Leon could make the simplest comment somehow sexual?

'Only to you,' she thought she heard him murmur, before he lifted a large bottle from the silver ice bucket. 'More champagne?' he offered urbanely, and refilled her glass. 'A toast to a beautiful woman and an impossible man.'

His black eyes met and held hers, a hint of challenge in their depths, and a wave of something very like fear washed over her. Until that moment she had succeeded in convincing herself that Leon was no longer a threat to her emotions. But, picking up her glass, then watching his long fingers curve around the stem of his own and lift it to his firmly chiselled mouth, she was not so sure.

'To partners,' Bea said firmly. She refused to be seduced by his brand of flirtation.

But her resolve was sorely tested when, after paying the bill, Leon waited until she was on her feet, and then slid a strong arm around her waist. The light of mockery dancing in his dark eyes, he bent his head and murmured, 'There, that wasn't so painful. Admit it, Phoebe,' and dropped a swift kiss on the top of her head.

Her immunity to Leon disappeared at the same speed as the masculine scent of him assailed her nostrils and the heat from his hard body seemed to engulf her. His fingers apparently idly kneaded her waist, but tightened perceptibly when she tried to move away.

'Lighten up, Phoebe. I am simply escorting you out of the restaurant. You look none too steady on those ridiculously high heels.'

Bea was not particularly tall, and she had worn the shoes in the faint hope that Leon would not tower over her quite so much, not to give him the excuse to hold her. 'They are not ridiculous, and I can walk by myself,' she snapped back.

'Temper fraying, sweet Phoebe?' Leon asked, a teasing light in his black eyes as he ushered her outside to where the car awaited them.

'No,' she denied, finally shrugging out of his hold. His soft chuckle did nothing for her temper. The trouble with Leon, Bea thought bitterly, was his complete and utter confidence in his masculine prowess. He knew exactly how he affected her, or any woman for that matter, and relished the knowledge.

'Not to worry, you'll soon be home now, and tucked up in your bed.' He opened the passenger door of the car, adding, 'Any chance of me doing the tucking, sweet Phoebe?'

She sent him one fulminating glance as she jumped into the passenger seat, and watched, appalled, as his dark head lowered. If he dared kiss her in a replay of the scene she had witnessed last night, she'd punch him on the nose. But he didn't. Instead he reached across her, carefully pulled out her seat belt and fastened it. Then he casually walked around the front of the car and slid into the driving seat.

'By your silence, Phoebe, I guess the answer is no,' Leon drawled with mock disappointment as she started the engine and drove off.

'Got it in one, buster, and why do you insist on calling me Phoebe?' Her exasperation and frustration finally spilled over. 'Everyone calls me Bea.'

'Bea does not suit you. When I think of a bee I think of an angry, buzzing yellow insect with a sting.' Taking his eyes from the road for a second, his glance slid over her flushed, angry face. His dark eyes gleamed briefly into hers. 'Then again, maybe it does. You certainly anger easily.' Turning his attention back to the road, he added, 'And I know you sting.'

'So call me Bea in future.' She did not like being compared to a stinging insect, but she preferred it to Phoebe.

'Never.'

'But why?' She cast him an exasperated glance. His clean-cut profile was illuminated by the glow from the streetlights, but shadows played over the rest of his face, masking any expression.

'The first time I ever saw you, as a young child, I was struck by how well your name suited you,' Leon responded quietly. 'I knew your name; your father, every time he came to our home in Cyprus, was always talking about his little girl. I can remember walking into your father's house in Northumbria, standing in the square hall and looking up at the large stained-glass window above the landing, halfway up the stairs. A single ray of sunlight was shining through it—a lot, given the state of English summers,' he opined with dry humour.

'Suddenly a tiny girl came whizzing backwards down the stairs, around the curve in the banister—a cloud of silver hair, a white dress and white legs. You shot to the bottom and fell. When you turned around the sun caught your face, and I saw you were truly a Phoebe. The name is from the Greek; it means shining, brilliant, and that is exactly what you were.'

'I don't remember that,' Bea said, oddly touched by his explanation.

'I'm not surprised. You landed on your behind and a second later you were bawling your eyes out. Aunt Lil swept you up against her ample bosom and carried you off.'

'Trust Lil,' Bea murmured fondly, letting her head fall back against the headrest. Heavens, she was tired.

'You're very loyal to those you trust, Phoebe. Which reminds me. I didn't have time to ask you on your birthday, but who or what gave you the idea I asked you to marry me simply to control your share of the company?'

Still dwelling on Leon's flattering explanation as to why he always called her by her proper name Bea wasn't paying much attention, and missed the underlying anger in his tone. 'It doesn't matter now. All water under the bridge, as they say.' She yawned widely, closing her eyes for a second, her previous late night catching up with her.

'Boring you, am I?'

The harshly spoken words made Bea sit up and take notice. They were parked outside her apartment block, the interior of the car illuminated by the overhead street-light. She glanced across at Leon. He was half turned towards her and his face was tight with anger; it glittered in his eyes.

'No, no, of course not,' she denied speedily. Although he no longer had the power to intimidate her, she saw no sense in provoking an argument. 'I have enjoyed our dinner date. But I had a very late night last night,' she offered by way of explanation.

'Your friend, Jack, keep you up all night, did he?' Leon asked crudely. 'Or should I say it?'

'Don't be so coarse,' Bea shot back. 'Just because you are incapable of having a platonic relationship with a member of the opposite sex, don't think everyone is the same. I have a lot of male friends, *friend* being the operative word. Not that it's any of your business.' Her mouth curled contemptuously. 'I certainly don't need advice on relationships from the Swashbuckling Tycoon.'

CHAPTER FIVE

HER words had found their mark. Leon, his eyes bleak and darkening with some emotion she could only guess at, said tersely, 'I apologise. The comment was uncalled for. But tell me, Phoebe, what did I ever do to you to give you such a terrible opinion of me? Surely you're intelligent enough to realise half of the stuff written about me is lies, or at the very least gross exaggeration?' A cynical smile twisted his hard lips. 'And, as I recall, three years ago it was *you* who dumped *me*. I was the innocent party, while you took your first step into love-them-and-leave-them mode.'

'Innocent?' Bea stared at him in amazement, wondering if the arrogant Leon Gregoris even knew the meaning of the word. He had probably lost his innocence not long after he'd left his mother's breast.

For a moment she was tempted to tell him the truth. That she knew all about Selina, the woman who had been his lover for years, the woman he had made pregnant *after* he had asked Bea to marry him and she had agreed. Agreed because Leon had played on her awakening sexuality like a virtuoso, exploiting her adolescent innocence until she was completely bemused by the sensual expertise of a sophisticated, experienced man and would have agreed to anything he asked of her.

Bea lowered her eyes from his enquiring gaze and bit her lip, remembering the most painful episode in her life to date. She wanted to blurt out her deep sense of betrayal, but the new, mature Bea had more sense. With hindsight she could almost feel sorry for Selina. Leon almost certainly would have paid for the child, but he had not done the honourable thing and married his long-time lover! No—Bea would not tell Leon the truth.

Instead, marshalling her thoughts, she said calmly, 'Contrary to what you imagine, I do not have a poor opinion of you, Leon. In fact I think you're an extremely astute businessman. In the past two weeks I have learned a lot about the company and, to be honest, I feel guilty owning thirty per cent. I don't deserve it. My father, and probably yours as well, was quite content to run a small, successful firm and earn a comfortable living. The reason it's such a success worldwide now, according to all the pundits, and confirmed by Tom Jordan, is entirely down to you. And I believe it. You're a genius in the financial world.'

It was the truth and Bea freely admitted it. Leon deserved the accolade where work was concerned; as for the rest, it really did not concern her. She had been hurt once by this man and she had learnt her lesson well: business and pleasure did not mix. Her blue eyes were cold when she finally raised them to meet his.

'But as for your private life, it has nothing to do with me.' Tonight it had been her turn to be wined and dined, but she had not forgotten that last night a different woman had been in the exact same position. 'And by the same token mine has nothing to do with you,' she concluded bluntly.

He watched her for a moment, and Bea didn't like the predatory look in his eyes. So, feigning an ease she did not feel, with a dismissive shrug she turned her back on him to release her safety belt. She tensed as his hand fell on her shoulder.

'Subject closed—just like that—?'

'I'm tired,' she cut in, without looking at him. 'Thank you for a lovely meal.'

His long fingers tightened on her naked shoulder, sending a tingling sensation down her spine. He was too large, too vitally male, and far, far too close. She held her breath as she felt those astute black eyes observing her intently in the dark interior of the car.

She heard the chiming of a clock in the distance and added a breathless, 'It's late. Goodnight.' Amazingly, he agreed…

'Okay, sweetheart.' With surprising alacrity Leon was out of the car, around the front and opening the passenger door before Bea had steadied her breathing.

'You do look tired, so I'll help you to your door.' His hand was once more on her shoulder, and he was guiding her across the pavement to the entrance hall of the apartment block before she recovered enough to speak.

'There's no—' She had been going to say 'no need', but never got the chance.

'In fact, although I'm not the most domesticated of men, in this instance I will even make the coffee you so obviously need…'

'Now, wait a minute…' But it was like trying to stop the tide. In moments they were outside her door, and Leon was demanding her key. 'I never invited you in for coffee,' she muttered, rooting in her bag for the key. She opened the door and turned. Leon's hand reached out and she stepped back instinctively. She didn't want him touching her again.

Leon smiled a rakish grin as he switched on the hall light. It gleamed on his night-black hair and threw the too handsome features into stark relief. 'Lead me to the kitchen, Phoebe, sweetheart.'

'Don't keep calling me sweetheart.' Bea swung on her heel, muttering under her breath. The man was too damn confident for his own good.

She was angry with herself for allowing him to steamroller his way into her apartment. Then she reminded herself it was *her* apartment. 'I suppose there's not much point in telling you I don't want any coffee and asking you to leave,' she said as she walked into the galley-style kitchen.

'None whatsoever. Go and sit down, relax. I can manage.'

She obeyed, simply because the alternative—staying in the confined space of the kitchen with Leon—was not appealing. Or maybe it was *too* appealing, a tiny voice echoed in her head.

Kicking off her shoes, she sat down on the sofa, curling her legs up beneath her. Her eyelids drooped, and she stifled another yawn.

'This is a first. A woman falling asleep on me,' a mocking voice drawled softly.

Forcing her eyes open, Bea looked up. 'What?' She yawned.

'Nothing important, Phoebe,' Leon said dryly as he stared down at her from his imposing height. He had shed his dinner jacket and got rid of his bow tie, and the top three buttons of his shirt were undone. He was enough to make any woman catch her breath. Then Bea noticed the tray in his hands.

'Coffee—you made it...' Her blue eyes widened in amazement. He had actually laid out two china cups and saucers, with her best silver cream jug, sugar bowl and coffee pot—a twenty-first birthday present from Lil and Bob, supposedly for her bottom drawer! A trousseau was an old-fashioned custom Bea did not believe in, and she hadn't used the coffee service.

'I am not the complete chauvinist you seem to think, Phoebe, as you will discover if you give me the chance.' And, bending, he placed the tray on the occasional table and sat down beside her. 'Shall I be mother?' he drawled, and proceeded to fill two cups from the coffee pot.

So much for a quick cup of instant and then turfing him out, as she had hoped, Bea thought. Sitting up straight, she slid her legs to the floor. 'Thank you,' she muttered, taking the cup and saucer Leon offered her. 'But it really wasn't necessary.'

'Not for you, maybe, but it is for me. Something you said in the car disturbed me, and, looking around this pleasant if small apartment, it occurred to me it's time we set the record straight.'

A puzzled frown creased Bea's smooth brow as she looked around the familiar room. His jacket and tie, draped over the armchair opposite, were the only items out of place. 'What has the size of my apartment got to do with anything?' she asked, and, taking a sip of her coffee, glanced sideways at Leon.

He tilted back his dark head and drained his cup. Bea was reluctantly fascinated by the subtle movement in the smooth column of his throat. He bent forward and replaced the empty cup on the tray. The fine silk of his shirt strained across his broad back, outlining muscle and sinew, the slight indentation of his spine, and Bea had to fight down an incredible urge to run her finger down it. She clasped her hands together in her lap. He was a magnificent male animal whichever way one looked at him, she realised, and she was no more immune to his charms than a million other females.

'It is a symptom of your father's upbringing,' Leon responded as he sat back, spreading his long arms along the back of the sofa. One of his hands was perilously near her shoulder. He stretched his long legs out in front of him with negligent ease, his feet crossed at the ankles. He looked as though he was settling in for a long stay.

'How much did your father tell you about the origin

of the firm?' he asked quietly, his dark head turned towards Bea, his black eyes seeking and holding hers.

'Do we have to…?' Bea began.

'Humour me this once, hmm?' Leon demanded quietly.

She eyed him warily, but there was no mistaking the serious intent in his expression. Bea allowed herself a nonchalant shrug. 'Okay.' The quicker she answered him, the sooner he would leave. 'Dad told me he was in the army and posted to Cyprus, where he met and made friends with your father. When Dad left the army, he spent a holiday in Cyprus with Nick, and between them they decided to set up in business—*ergo* Stephen-Gregoris. It's no great secret.'

'It wasn't quite that simple. Your father saved my father's life. My father got into a bar-room brawl, and your father intervened and took the knife meant for my dad's heart in his forearm.'

Bea's eyes widened; she was intrigued. 'So that's where he got his scar!' she exclaimed. As a child it had fascinated her—the long, ragged slash down her father's arm. He had explained it as a battle scar—the result of ten years in the army.

'Yes, but there's more. The company flourished quite well for a number of years, until the Turks invaded the island in 1974. I was a boy at the time, and we lived in Northern Cyprus—the part that is now controlled by Turkey. My father lost almost everything, and once again your father came to the rescue. He supported both families for a while, until they could get the business going again. As a precaution they decided to set up the head office on the Greek mainland, in Athens; it seemed a safer bet and it looks like proving to be correct. Unfortunately there's trouble brewing again in Cyprus.'

Bea had seen the news and knew there had been a

skirmish recently, but it seemed to have quietened down again—though for how long was anybody's guess. But she was in no mood to discuss the political situation in Cyprus, or anywhere else. 'Why are you telling me all this?' she asked, because she really did not see the point.

'Because earlier you said you felt guilty at owning so many shares in what is now a very large concern.' His voice was almost terse. 'Don't ever think like that again, Phoebe. You are entitled to everything you have, and more. Our fathers were partners, and it was because of your father's trust and loyalty that the company continued to flourish. If it hadn't been for him I wouldn't be where I am today,' Leon opined hardily. 'The debt my family owes yours is unquantifiable.'

'I think you're rather overstating the case,' she said awkwardly. The passionate intensity in Leon's tone was so unlike his usual light-heartedness.

'No, it's how I feel. I am Greek and I promised my father on his deathbed that I would always honour the debt of gratitude and abiding friendship between our two families, that I would always look after you. So never again let me hear you say you do not deserve your wealth.'

He glanced at his watch, and Bea noticed again that it was an expensive gold one—but then everything about Leon was expensive. Hard on the heels of the thought, she frowned and looked around the simple room.

'Understand, Phoebe.' His harsh demand brought her eyes back to his face. 'Last night, if I appeared a little too concerned about you and your friend, now you know why. I have difficulty remembering you're a grown woman, but I am trying,' he said with a wry grimace. 'Though beware, Phoebe, I will never stop protecting you, if I consider you need it.'

'Now why does that worry me?' she jibed. The

thought of Leon looking after her was horrific, yet oddly comforting.

'Don't worry. I learnt my lesson when I tried to marry you to protect you.' She sensed the derision behind his words. 'First I thought you called it off because I was too old for you, but then I discovered it was because you didn't trust me. I hope after our little chat tonight you realise you can trust me, and why?'

He was astute, Bea acknowledged. She knew he had tried to marry her to consolidate his hold over the business, and he had failed. Now he was smoothly suggesting it had been friendship and his promise to a dying man to protect her that had prompted their brief engagement. The truth was probably somewhere in between, but Bea was not about to delve into that particular morass. Instead she simply said, 'Yes, of course, Leon.'

'Thank you,' he drawled mockingly. 'Such enthusiasm is quite overwhelming.'

The old Leon was back. His black eyes gleamed with devilment as he shifted his long legs and moved closer, allowing his arm to fall from the back of the sofa and encircle her slender waist. Bea was trapped between his arm and Leon's muscular thigh, hard against her own. Immediately she felt a burning sensation through the thin fabric of her dress. She felt his muscles tense and wondered for a second if it was because he felt the same sexual heat that afflicted her.

'Now we've got that settled, Phoebe, let me give you some advice.'

Obviously not the same affliction, Bea thought, maddened. Leon sounded as cool as a cucumber while she felt hot and flustered. He was back to being his arrogant self, dishing out advice whether she wanted it or not.

'Seriously, as your friend and partner, I am telling you

never to feel guilty about money. It is not a sin to be rich, or to enjoy oneself.'

She tried to inch away, but the grip of her waist tightened. 'You're suggesting I should stop worrying about money and start spending it?' The gleam in his eyes did not resemble the caring light of a true friend giving advice. More likely it was a very astute masculine awareness of exactly how he affected her.

'Well put.' Leon grinned, and, lifting one long finger, he slipped it under the halter neck of her dress. 'This is a lovely dress, and you look gorgeous in anything.' His eyes appraised her with deliberate slowness from head to foot. 'But you can afford to be clothed by the best designers in the world.'

'Maybe I don't want to…to be…' she stuttered, her nerves quivering in response to his nearness.

'Then look at this apartment. Your father was a cautious man, but it's a different situation now, Phoebe. Buy yourself a penthouse, if you want.'

'Like you, you mean,' she said coldly, but her flesh burnt where his finger idly stroked her breastbone. She could feel her nipples tighten into hard buds of arousal and prayed he would not drop his gaze and discover her embarrassment. Jerking forward, she placed the cup she was still grasping on the table, dislodging his marauding fingers at the same time.

'I don't actually own a penthouse,' Leon remarked, a hint of amusement in his tone. 'The company owns all the apartments in Athens, New York and Hong Kong. My one indulgence is cars. I keep a Maserati in Athens, a Ferrari in New York, a Mercedes in London and a Jaguar in Hong Kong. But the only house I own is the villa in Cyprus.'

Bea believed him. Leon always had to be in control. The thought of another person driving him anywhere was probably anathema to him. 'Where do you stay in London?' she queried, wondering how much longer it would take to get rid of him. The hand at her waist hadn't slackened its grip, and it was taking all her strength to remain perched on the edge of the sofa.

'I'm not very often in London, and when I am I stay with a good friend or at the Dorchester.'

The 'good friend' is a woman, no doubt, she thought, but did not say it. 'Nice for you,' she said, glancing back at him over her shoulder.

'Nice for you too, Phoebe. Technically the properties are yours as much as mine—feel free to use them any time.'

'Speaking of time, it is eleven and I'm bushed.'

'Your late night is catching up with you,' Leon drawled mockingly, letting go of her waist and getting to his feet. 'Okay, I don't want to outstay my welcome.'

What welcome? Bea thought, and immediately felt guilty. He wasn't a bad man. Her eyes followed him as, in a few lithe strides, he crossed the room and reached for his jacket. He was just an incorrigible flirt and so irresistible with it!

Turning towards her, he hesitated briefly, not quite his usual confident self. He glanced down at her.

'I'll call around about ten in the morning; we can spend the day together.'

'Sorry, I can't. I'm going out.' She saw him stiffen, but ploughed on—though she didn't owe him an explanation. 'It was arranged last night. My friend Nan is down for the weekend and Jack suggested we all go to Brighton for the day. It should be fun.' Bea saw no reason to tell Leon that Nan was Jack's girlfriend.

Leon dropped his jacket and took a step forward.

'There's an antiques fair on. I thought I might buy

something,' she babbled on, the atmosphere in the room suddenly fraught with tension.

Temper flashed briefly in his eyes, and was almost immediately overlaid by something much more sinister. He lowered his large body down onto the sofa beside her again, and lifted a hand to slide it once more around her waist. 'In that case I must make the most of tonight.'

'Thank you for tonight.' Bea battled on politely, wishing desperately that he would leave. She looked frantically round the room, anywhere but at Leon. His hand had crept up to the underside of her breast and her body was betraying her yet again. He was just so damn smooth! She could leap up like an outraged virgin, but she didn't want to give him the chance to laugh at her. Her gaze alighted on a flower vase. 'Oh, and I forgot to thank you for the roses and the groceries you bought for me when I first arrived here.'

'My pleasure. But the one thing I really want I find I cannot buy,' Leon said enigmatically, lying back against the soft cushions, looking for all the world as if he was settling in for the night.

Resolutely she resisted the subtle pressure of his hand on her side, tempting her to fall back against him. She could feel his breath on her bare back and she shivered, but not from the cold. Folding her arms over her chest to disguise her peaked nipples, she rabbited on, 'Yes, well, I'm sure you'll find a way. You always do. But, if you don't mind, I want to go to bed.'

His deep-throated chuckle did amazing things to her heartbeat. He bent his head, sliding his free hand into the thickness of her hair and brushing it to one side. Then she felt the warmth of his mouth on the nape of her neck and she shivered again. 'Sweet Phoebe. I want to go to bed as well.' The husky words brushed against the soft whorls of her ear.

Bea sucked in her breath and stiffened her back ramrod-straight. 'So go!' she snapped. She might have known he would make a pass. He couldn't help himself.

'Relax,' Leon drawled. 'I have to leave on Monday afternoon and so, as tomorrow is out, we must make the most of tonight. Remember what I told you earlier. You're a grown woman now. Let's enjoy ourselves together.'

Angrily she turned her head towards him. His lips curled into a smile as he caught her half-smothered denial with his mouth.

His lips against hers silenced her, and his hand held her head still beneath his. His other hand slid up her back, holding her closer to his broad chest. He deepened the kiss, letting her feel the possessive heat of his passion. Bea tried to remain immune to his assault on her senses but old memories, never far from the surface, welled up inside her, bringing with them the familiar rush of desire only Leon seemed able to arouse in her.

Her arms curved up and around his shoulders of their own volition. She felt her breasts crushed softly against the muscular wall of his chest, and suddenly she was responding helplessly to the promise of his lips. His tongue surged in her mouth as his fingers slipped the tie of her halter-necked dress. Her head fell back and she gasped as she felt his fingers trail down her throat and delve beneath the lacy edge of her strapless bra, grazing across her nipples.

Her slender body trembled in his hold and she only vaguely realised when her legs left the floor. She was held firmly in his lap by one strong arm while his free hand dealt with the front fastening of her bra.

Finally Leon lifted his head and stared down into her flushed, bemused face. There was a dark, demanding hunger in his eyes that stilled her frantically racing pulse.

'Leon, I don't think this a good...' Bea began.

'I want you...and I know you want me. Let me show you true pleasure,' he rasped throatily, his glittering eyes raking her beautiful face and then dropping to her firm, high breasts. His head swooped down, his tongue licking over each taut nipple in turn.

Bea bit her lip against the exquisite sensations flooding through her body. 'No,' she gasped in dismay, appalled by her own swift surrender.

'Yes,' he contradicted her, and bit lightly on her breast before raising his head and kissing her fleetingly. 'Don't think, feel. The chemistry between us has always been there, whatever else went wrong.' His large hand cupped the lush weight of her breast, his thumb grazing the aching tip. His dark, knowing gaze flicked from her face to her breast and back, to emphasise his point. 'You know it's true, Phoebe. Let's give ourselves a chance, see where it leads.'

Bea wanted to. She had never wanted anything so much in her life. But she knew where it would lead, she thought sadly: to disgust with herself and to another notch on Leon's belt.

As if sensing her uncertainty, suddenly Leon moved, turning her under him. She was trapped by his arms at either side of her and his large hands threaded through her long hair, framing her face, holding her head gently between his palms. His mouth closed over hers once more, hot and passionate, his tongue plunging its moist secret depths.

Bea was made achingly aware of the full weight of his rock-hard arousal, moving against her belly in rhythm with his mind-drugging kiss. She could barely breathe, but didn't care. Frantically her small hands slid beneath his open shirt and tangled in the soft hair of his broad chest, her fingers brushing a hard male nipple.

Leon groaned against her mouth and trailed a string of kisses down her throat and lower, until his dark head nestled between her breasts. Then he was suckling on their hardened tips, first one and then the other. A low moan escaped her, arrows of pleasure darting from her breasts to the apex of her thighs. She quivered helplessly as his mouth moved, tasting her skin. Her back arched, encouraging his ministrations even as some tiny corner of her rational mind reminded her he was an expert in the sexual stakes, and a confirmed womaniser.

But when he lifted his head and their glances collided Bea read the question in the fiery depths of his eyes. She saw the skin pulled taut across his cheekbones with desire, the dark flush on his tanned face. She also knew it didn't matter. She wanted him.

Bea reached a hand to his square chin, hypnotised by the undiluted hunger in his fiery gaze. Tonight he wanted her…only her… She traced his jawline and felt the beginnings of stubble. He always had been a hairy man. Her childhood hero. A soft smile curved her mouth, and Leon took it for assent.

'Phoebe.' His voice was a husky groan. 'You're so beautiful, so passionate, and God knows I've waited so long.' His hot mouth found hers once more, and they were swept up in a swirling tide of passion.

Leon's hands and mouth roamed over her body, stroking, kissing, and she needed no urging to return his caresses. Her fingers teased his chest hair, again discovered the hard male nipples, stroked his broad shoulders and tangled in the silky black hair of his head. She was delirious with excitement and pleasure.

'You're sure?' Leon demanded gutturally, easing her skirt up around her waist. He moulded her hips with his hands and slid between her thighs.

Blue eyes bravely holding black, slowly she lowered

her hands to the waistband of his trousers, her fingers finding the clasp. Bea felt his sharp intake of breath and the flex of his stomach muscles. The silence was laced with a sexual tension so acute, she could taste it. The musky scent of his powerful male body filled her nostrils. The clasp was undone... Bea hesitated, suddenly shy, then her fingers found the top of the zip, her knuckles brushing against hard, bulging male flesh. Leon groaned—a hoarse, aching sound...

Then the doorbell rang.

Bea's hand dropped from the zip. 'The door,' she murmured. 'Someone's at the door.'

'Ignore it,' Leon rasped, catching her hand in his and lowering it to his thigh as his mouth once more took hers.

The ringing continued. 'Leon, I must answer,' Bea murmured against his mouth, and, pushing against his chest with her small hands, she tried to wriggle free.

The bell rang again. 'Who the hell calls this late anyway?' Leon demanded, frustration lacing his voice, but he let her up.

Shocked by what she had almost allowed to happen, Bea staggered to her feet, her heart pounding and her legs like jelly.

'Wait!' Leon snapped, and she stood before him meek as a child as with swift expertise he fastened her bra and retied the halter of her dress. 'We don't want your late-night guest shocked out of their socks, do we?' he said.

Bea stared at him. The man mad with passion only minutes ago was now in complete control, and she felt like a quivering wreck. But then Leon was a past master at getting women in and out of their clothes—and why not? He had certainly had plenty of practice, she thought bitterly, and, swinging on her heel, she dived for the hall and the front door.

'Saved by the bell,' she muttered under her breath, and flung open the door.

'Hi, Bea. I saw your light on when I arrived and thought, Great! It's not yet midnight.' Margot walked past Bea into the small hall. 'I can't wait to find out how your heavy date went last night.'

Bea closed the door and, turning, stopped Margot from strolling into the living room with a hand on her arm. 'Still living vicariously, are we?' she teased—anything to delay her friend for a moment. It had suddenly hit Bea: she had left Leon standing with his shirt undone, his trousers half undone and with no jacket on. Silently she prayed he had had time to get dressed as she listened to Margot chatter on.

'Well, as it happens, I woke up at the crack of dawn and did catch a glimpse of you staggering out of a taxi with an incredibly attractive Latin-looking young man.' Margot walked on into the sitting room, heading for the kitchen with Bea reluctantly following her. 'I want to hear all the juicy details over a cup of cocoa, and—Mr Gregoris!' Margot exclaimed, stopping dead.

Bea hardly dared look at him, but when she did it wasn't too bad. Leon was standing by the fireplace. His shirt and trousers were fastened, and his jacket was draped casually over his arm. Only the bow tie was still missing.

'Hello, Margot. I'm glad to see you're taking such an interest in our young charge.' Leon looked across at Bea, a cynical light in his dark eyes. 'And I wouldn't mind hearing all the juicy details myself. An incredibly attractive Latin-looking young man, you say? How interesting,' he drawled silkily. 'I can see I shall have to keep a closer eye on my young partner.'

Bea bristled at the word 'young', and could guess what he was thinking. Leon had left her with Jack, a tall blond, and she had ended up with Andy, someone quite different. But Leon was as bad. No, worse, she thought scathingly. He had no right to take this moral tone with her. A picture of his model friend formed in her mind, and gave her the courage to reply carelessly, 'That was Andy, a really rather nice man. Something in the City, I think.'

But Margot seemed to have lost interest. Instead she was looking from one to the other of them, a thoughtful expression on her face. She turned to Bea. 'Sorry. I didn't mean to intrude. You should have told me you had a visitor.'

'Oh, please, Margot, stay. Mr Gregoris took me out to dinner, but it was strictly business. You're not intruding at all—in fact Leon was just leaving.' She glanced up at Leon defiantly. 'Weren't you?' she demanded, her blue eyes daring him to disagree.

'Yes, of course. I'll leave you two to your gossip.' Leon bent and casually picked his bow tie up from the arm of the chair, dangling it provocatively between his long fingers. Bea could have slapped him... But he wasn't looking at her. He was saying goodnight to Margot. Then, turning to Bea, with a wicked gleam in his dark eyes, he added, 'As it happens I have a rather pressing problem I had hoped to solve tonight. Show me to the door, Phoebe. Perhaps you can help me.'

Bea's face flamed. He was back with the innuendos. She only hoped Margot didn't realise it. Marching into the hall, she made for the door, her hand going out to open it.

'Wait a second,' Leon ordered hardily, trapping her hand with his. She glanced up at him in the dimly lit hallway. His face was in shadow, but there was no mistaking the determination in his eyes.

'Put your jacket on and go,' Bea said flatly.

'In a minute, but first you owe me, lady,' he hissed, pressing her hand beneath his folded jacket. 'Feel what you do to me.' Bea's face burned even more as he forced her hand flat against his still aroused male flesh. Now she understood why his jacket was draped strategically over his arm, and she quickly pulled her hand free.

'It's not my fault you're an over-sexed womaniser,' she hissed back, keeping her voice low. It was a very small apartment and sound carried. No way did she want Margot hearing the conversation.

'I gave up my womanising ways the day I realised it was possible to have an erection and be bored at the same time. I am much more discerning now, and I don't appreciate being led to the brink and left cold.'

Bea tried to choke back a totally unsuitable desire to laugh, and failed. 'Cold,' she chuckled, her blue eyes lit with laughter and clashing with Leon's. He was anything but cold! She could feel his heat reaching out to her.

His firm lips twitched and he couldn't suppress an answering grin. 'You think it funny, you little tease?' Ruefully he shook his head. 'One day, Phoebe, one day... Be warned, I am going to have you, and when I do you won't be laughing, but begging.' And, dropping a gentle kiss on the top of her head, he let himself out.

Dream on, buster, Bea thought, dismissing her earlier weakness as simply tiredness and proximity to a lethally attractive man. She was over Leon now, she reminded herself as she walked back into the living room.

Margot was standing in the doorway of the kitchen, a mug of cocoa in each hand. She burst into a hurried apology. 'Bea, I feel such a fool barging in like that; I'm so sorry. But it never entered my head that Leon Gregoris could be here, and I realise it should have done. After all, you are his business partner, even if you do seem just like one of the workers.'

'Can it, Margot,' Bea said bluntly, and collapsed onto the sofa. The last thing she wanted was for Margot to start seeing her as a boss figure, and with that in mind she gave her a carefully edited account of the evening. 'Leon was doing his usual heavy uncle act. Checking up on me to make sure I'm behaving myself and working hard. Nothing more.'

'Are you sure?' Margot asked, handing Bea a mug of steaming cocoa and sitting down in the armchair opposite. 'Do you mind if I speak frankly?' Margot went on, eyeing Bea's messed-up hair with a wry smile.

'Of course not.' Bea grinned at her friend. She had quickly realised Margot was outspoken to the point of bluntness. 'Why change the habit of a lifetime?' she quipped, and took a sip of the warm chocolate.

'I'm a lot older than you, Bea, and a lot more worldly, shall we say. Leon Gregoris is a very charismatic, powerful man, but if he has one fault it is women. Notice the plural, and beware. According to office gossip over the years, he only ever once got close to committing to a woman, and even that fizzled out. I'm warning you, Bea. From what I sensed tonight, when I walked in here, Leon Gregoris in no way sees himself as your uncle.'

'Well, that's how I see him,' Bea said flatly, gulping down the rest of her cocoa. Carefully she put the mug back on the table and glanced at Margot. 'Don't you start worrying about me as well, Margot. I can look after myself. Take last night, for instance.'

In a swift change of subject Bea gave Margot an exaggerated version of the previous evening. She described the hilarity of Leon being locked in the loo, and gave the impression they had parted at the office. Then she went on to describe her great night out with her friends. And if she accentuated Andy's charms while avoiding mentioning Leon's part in the evening, what did it matter? Finally, when she'd told Margot her plans for a day out in Brighton with Jack, Nan and Andy tomorrow, the older woman got up to leave, totally convinced Bea had her life well under control.

Bea went to bed telling herself the same thing, and the next morning, when she climbed into the back of Andy's Range Rover with the rest of her friends, she was convinced of it.

Brighton was a roaring success, and they finally returned to London just before midnight.

Bea jumped out of the Range Rover into Andy's open arms, and quite enjoyed his kiss. The ribald comments from her friends made her laugh, and she was still laughing as Andy showed her to her door.

She might not have been as happy if she had noticed the black car parked on the opposite side of the road. Or the thunderous expression on the face of its driver...

CHAPTER SIX

ON MONDAY morning Bea eyed the contents of her wardrobe with a frown. Leon was right; she should splash out a bit on clothes. Apart from a handful of dresses, she only had two outfits for work: the blue suit she had worn on Friday and a simple black suit in almost exactly the same style. She glanced out of the window. It was a beautiful sunny day, not a cloud in the sky, and suddenly she decided to hell with the suit, took one of her favourite dresses out of the closet and crossed to the dressing-table mirror.

She slipped the dress over her head and smoothed it down over her thighs. She eyed her reflection. Not quite...she mused. Then quickly she opened a drawer and took out a gold Chanel belt. She slung it around her hips and it immediately lifted the soft forest-green shift, with its tiny sleeves and slightly scooped neck, from simple to stylish—in the process shortening even further its already short straight skirt. She smiled at her reflection in the mirror, well satisfied with the result.

Bea breezed into the office half an hour later with Margot, not for a second admitting to herself that she had dressed with more care than usual because Leon might appear.

Appear he did. Bea had not even made it to her little office before he burst out of Tom Jordan's. 'What time do you call this, ladies?' His dark eyes swept over Bea from head to toe, narrowing slightly on the hemline of her skirt and her shapely legs.

Bea opened her mouth to speak, but Margot answered. 'Eight-twenty, Mr Gregoris. We're ten minutes early.'

With a hard look at Bea, Leon switched his attention to Margot. 'Never mind, get in here. We have work to do.'

'Good morning to you too,' Bea muttered, opening the door to her office. What or who had rattled his cage? she wondered as she switched on her computer and sat down at her desk.

Two minutes later her door was flung open. 'What is keeping you?' Leon growled.

Bea looked up. 'I—I didn't realise you meant me,' she stuttered, the fierceness of his expression temporarily unnerving her.

'You never do,' he grated inexplicably. Leaning against the door, he added, 'Move it,' and waited for her to walk past.

The morning was a revelation. Bea had always known Leon was clever, but watching him in action was an education. He created an electric atmosphere simply by his presence; power and dynamism radiated from him.

Seated at Tom's desk, Leon quickly went through the turnover of the London office. In rapid succession he spoke to the Athens and New York offices. Bea felt sorry for the poor person in America. It was a little after midday in London and, given the time difference, it had to be the crack of dawn there.

Tom and Margot hovered around, answering all Leon's questions and immediately implementing his suggestions. Bea's role turned out to be the coffee-maker, but she didn't mind; it was fascinating to see Leon at work.

Finally Leon stood up. 'A quick lunch before I have to leave. Tom, you'll join me?'

Bea hid a flicker of disappointment behind a bright

smile. 'Well, if you'll excuse me, I must get on with my own work.' She started for the door.

'Phoebe, the *four* of us are going to eat.' And then, turning his attention to Margot, he said, 'Get Reception to hold all calls until later, and let's get out of here.'

Over a light meal of pasta and salad Leon sought their views on the Far East. The discussion that ensued, on the advantages of trading with the Pacific Rim economies and how Leon intended to exploit them, left Bea speechless with admiration. An hour later they were heading back for the office.

Leon said goodbye to Tom and Margot but, grasping Bea's hand, he prevented her from following them inside. The kiss he bestowed on her parted lips left her speechless for quite another reason.

'Behave yourself. I'll be in touch,' he said, and was sliding into his car and gone before Bea could get her breath back.

She looked guiltily around, terrified that anyone she knew might have seen her, but the flow of people walking along the pavement was devoid of any familiar faces. She must stop Leon doing that! she told herself for the umpteenth time. But without much hope of success...

Sighing, she walked into the building and entered the lift. Sophie, the receptionist, was standing with her finger on the 'hold' button.

'Aiming a bit high, aren't you?' she said in her cool voice.

Bea blushed to the roots of her hair. Obviously Sophie had seen the kiss and had drawn her own conclusion. Bea couldn't say she liked the girl. She was the sort of woman who sparkled around the male sex but seemed to have little time for her own. But maybe Bea was being unkind; she didn't really know Sophie.

'I'm not aiming anywhere,' she finally said, forcing a smile as the lift moved. 'It was just a bit of fun.'

'So long as you remember that. Leon Gregoris is a great lover, but don't get any ideas. His sort will never marry a working girl. If he ever does marry, it will be to some filthy-rich society babe. Believe me, I know.' The trace of bitterness in her tone was undeniable.

'You're probably right,' Bea agreed, suddenly feeling inexplicably low. It was a relief to walk out of the elevator and reach the sanctuary of her own office. Sophie's comments shouldn't have got to her, but they had. Obviously the woman was another notch on Leon's belt.

Summer gave way to autumn—not that it was very noticeable in the heart of the city. In the weeks since Leon had left Bea had settled into an enjoyable routine.

Leon called her very occasionally at her apartment, from wherever he happened to be in the world, and always at the most ungodly hour, Bea thought with a wry smile as she sat down at her desk one day. More often she spoke to him at the office, when he rang to speak to Tom and she put his call through. She was quietly proud of her ability to manage these telephone conversations with a degree of efficiency and sophistication.

Another Monday, but she wasn't blue, and it had nothing to do with the fact that she had spoken to Leon last night. She glanced at her wristwatch. He should be in Hong Kong now, she mused, and on Saturday he would be back in England.

'Penny for them,' Margot said, walking up to her desk. 'You looked rapt. Dreaming about Andy, were you?'

Margot had met the young man and liked him, so Bea simply smiled, and said, 'Jealous?'

'Too young for me. Though when you're through with him I might fancy taking on a toy boy.'

'And what about your financial friend?' She tilted her head back. 'Up there.'

That was all it took to get Margot talking about her boyfriend and forgetting about Bea's love life.

By Thursday morning every little bit of information of the previous weekend's escapades was talked out, and relative calm reigned. But not for long...

'Bea.' It was a softly spoken word, and Bea's head jerked up from the program she was working on and she smiled. But quickly her smile turned to a worried frown.

Tom Jordan was standing in her doorway. Today he looked as if the weight of the world had fallen on his shoulders, and not a glimmer of humour lit his blue eyes.

'Come into my office, Bea,' he demanded quietly. 'We need to talk.'

The fact that he had come looking for her instead of simply ringing through was ominous enough, but the expression on his face was worse. Slowly Bea got to her feet and silently followed Tom through to his office. His curt command to Margot to hold all calls had Bea racking her brain for what disastrous mistake she must have made to be personally summoned in such a way.

'Sit down, Bea.'

She did. 'What have I done?' she blurted.

Tom, instead of sitting at his desk, pulled up a chair to face hers. 'Now, I don't want you to get upset, or worried...' he began earnestly.

Of course his words had completely the opposite effect on Bea. Her heart stopped. It had to be personal. 'Lil and Bob.' She said the names of the only two people she was close to. 'What's happened? An accident?' she asked, the colour draining from her face.

'No, no, nothing like that. Everything will be fine. But we have a bit of a problem.'

Bea breathed more easily. 'A problem?' she queried.

'I have just had a telephone call from head office in Athens. Apparently they were informed yesterday by the Hong Kong office that Leon has been kidnapped.'

'Kidnapped? Leon?' She couldn't help it; she started to chuckle—it had to be a joke. 'No one would have the nerve!' she exclaimed. She didn't believe it for a minute. She glanced at Tom, expecting him to share her amusement, but was shocked into silence by the grim expression on his face.

'Unfortunately, it's true. He's been kidnapped.'

'Kidnapped,' she repeated, like a parrot.

Reaching out, Tom took her small hands in his in a gesture of comfort. 'It seems he arrived in Hong Kong on Monday and drove out to stay with a friend in the New Territories for the night. He was supposed to be in the office on Tuesday, but never arrived. Instead a ransom note was delivered. The kidnappers want twenty million pounds. The demand was accompanied by a distinctive gold keyring, with the keys to his Jaguar attached, and, more ominously, a lock of wavy black human hair. The police were informed.'

'It could be anyone's keys or hair,' Bea said slowly, refusing to believe what she was hearing.

'The police have checked with the friend Leon spent the night with. It is Leon's keyring and it is European hair—not Asian; apparently there is a difference.'

'Oh, my God!' The full enormity of what Tom was telling her was beginning to sink in.

'The Hong Kong police are almost sure a Triad gang is responsible, and, while they will do everything in their power to find Leon, they suggest the money be prepared just in case. I don't know if you have ever been to Hong

Kong, but it's like a rabbit warren—trying to find one
man must be extremely difficult. As the police said, the
car would be more difficult to hide than the man.'

'So what are we going to do?' she demanded, panic
edging her tone. 'I'll go there straight away. I'll get the
next flight. No, the company jet.' Bea tried to rise, but
Tom's hand forced her to remain seated.

'No, Bea, you must stay here. In fact a detective inspector from New Scotland Yard will be arriving at
eleven to interview you.'

'Interview me?' She couldn't understand what was
happening. 'Why me?'

'That's the part I'm coming to. You know your father
and Leon's were great friends, and I know what your
father would do now if he was alive. But I don't want
to put pressure on you in any way. It has to be your
decision.'

'For heaven's sake, Tom, what are you going on
about?' If Tom had one fault, it was his inability to get
to the point.

'Twenty million is a huge amount of money. Stephen-
Gregoris is a highly successful company, but it does
have to consider its shareholders. In most kidnap cases
an appeal to the family would probably apply. But
there's no point in asking Leon's stepmother, because
her income is tied up to Leon's share of the company.
So, for there to be any chance of assembling the money
quickly, the head office in Athens need your consent. As
the single biggest shareholder, next to Leon, basically
it's your decision whether to pay up or not.'

'Yes, yes, of course—anything, Tom. What is money
when a man's life is at stake?' Now she understood his
remarks about her father. 'I'm surprised you need to
ask.'

'I knew you would agree; you're a good kid, Bea.'

Standing up, he added, 'I'll get on the blower to Greece and set the wheels in motion.'

The rest of the day was a blur to Bea. She signed documents, banker's drafts—anything Tom put in front of her—and the inspector from New Scotland Yard arrived. He told her he was questioning her on behalf of the Hong Kong police and said that sometimes business partners knew more than most about each other. But Bea was no help. How could she be? She still didn't really believe it had happened. Leon in captivity was unthinkable.

But when the detective insisted on absolute secrecy, informing her that only three members of staff in Hong Kong were aware of the kidnap, in Greece only two people—the company lawyer and the director of head office—and in Britain only Tom Jordan and herself, and that it had to stay that way, it finally hit Bea just how perilous the situation was.

She jumped to her feet and paced agitatedly around Tom's office, her mind in a whirl. She suggested again flying out to Hong Kong, but neither Tom nor the police would hear of it.

'But when they find him he'll want to be met by a friend, at the very least,' Bea cried, the full horror of what had happened finally cutting through the fog in her brain. Then her imagination took over: Leon alone, in chains, in the dark, maybe already dead. It was a nightmare. 'I must do something. Go there.'

Tom put an arm around her shoulders. 'No, Bea. Your place is here. When Leon is free he won't be alone; you forget he was staying with long-time friends the night before he was taken. They'll be waiting for him just as anxiously as us.'

Tom was right, she realised sadly, and, knowing Leon, there was probably a lovely lady there somewhere too.

'All right,' she finally conceded, and, rubbing her bare arms, trying to instil some heat into her numb flesh, she sank back down on the chair.

Then the detective inspector told her that, as a precaution, she would be kept under surveillance for her own protection until the situation was resolved satisfactorily. The Triad organisation had long tentacles and was known to be active in London. She voiced no protest; she was frozen in shock.

Bea didn't want to leave the office that night, but Tom insisted she go home. Perhaps the worst part of all was that she couldn't talk about it to anyone; the information was strictly on a need-to-know basis, and even Margot hadn't been informed.

Ensconced in her small apartment, Bea paced the floor for hours on end. She telephoned Lil at home, but for Lil and Bob's sake she had to pretend everything was fine, when really she was crying inside. She couldn't eat, she couldn't sleep. Tom had promised to ring if there were any developments, and she lay in bed, her ears straining to hear the telephone.

On Friday lunchtime, Margot demanded, 'Come on, Bea, I'm not a fool. Something has happened to upset both you and Tom. You never said a word all the way to the office, and you've sat at that desk all morning watching the telephone and jumping out of your skin every time it rings. What's wrong?'

Bea looked at her friend with haunted eyes. 'Nothing—nothing at all—'

'Leave her alone, Margot,' Tom Jordan broke in sternly, walking into the office. 'It's a private matter and not to be discussed.' The tone of his voice was enough to warn Margot not to question further.

By Sunday Bea was quietly going out of her mind. She hadn't left her apartment all weekend. She was tormented by thoughts of what Leon must be going through.

Leon had always been such an active man, he'd used to run morning and night, and probably still did—when he was free. In the villa in Paphos the basement was his own personal gym. One only had to look at his physique to see it was honed to the peak of fitness. She had nightmares about his beautiful body, broken and bent.

She went to bed, but she didn't sleep through a whole night.

Leon might be a rake, a womaniser, but he was her friend. She forgot all her bitterness over their broken engagement, and remembered only the good times. How as a child she had adored him—his stupid rhymes and his wacky sense of humour. He had always been there for her; at her father's funeral his had been the comforting shoulder to cry on, and as her trustee he had taken care of everything for her. And then, on her twenty-first birthday, he had handed her inheritance to her with a smile and a present of a pendant, and she had never really thanked him for any of it.

Next morning Bea did something she hadn't done for years. She knelt by the side of the bed and, her slender hands clasped together, offered up a silent prayer for his safe return. Childishly she promised God anything, if only Leon was safe.

She did the same every day until finally, the next Thursday, her prayer was answered.

The call came through from Hong Kong just as Bea was about to leave the office after another futile day of waiting. It was the middle of the night in Hong Kong; the hand-over of the cash had been arranged, the police had been waiting and it had all gone smoothly. The kidnappers were caught, the money recovered and Leon had been discovered, gagged and chained to a wall, in a small compartment only two feet by four.

Ten days confined in such a way had taken their toll, but a doctor had seen him and declared there was no permanent damage. He was all right and recovering in a private clinic, and would be in touch after a debriefing by the police.

Tom declared a celebratory drink was in order, and, with Margot finally let in on the story, the three of them retired to the nearest wine bar and got very merry.

Bea's sense of euphoria lasted until the next morning.

After a good night's sleep she skipped out of the apartment block with Margot, eager to get to work, sure that Leon would call to speak to Tom, if not her.

He did. 'Phoebe—Leon here.'

The sound of his voice over the phone was music to her ears. Her eyes filmed with moisture. 'Leon. Oh, thank God. It's so good to hear your voice. Are you all right? I won't believe it until I see you again. When will you be here? I was almost worried out of my mind.' She knew she was babbling, but it was such a relief.

'No need to worry, Phoebe, I'm fine—and so is your money. I believe I have you to thank for allowing the ransom to go ahead.'

'It was nothing. I'm just so glad you got away unharmed.'

'Twenty million is quite something to most people,' Leon drawled cynically. 'Thank you again. Now, put me through to Tom; I don't have time to gossip.'

'Yes, yes, of course.' Bea did as he said. She should have been happy; Leon was fine, she had spoken to him. But something was wrong.

Bea sat staring blankly at her console, chewing on her bottom lip. It was Leon, but it wasn't. Gone was the humorous chat, the not so subtle innuendo; he had sounded curt almost to the point of rudeness. Reluctantly she turned her attention to the document on the screen. She was supposed to be working, not worrying about Leon, she told herself firmly. But somehow her earlier euphoria on learning of his safe return gave way to a feeling of anticlimax.

You're rotten, she remonstrated with herself. Leon was fine; he had spoken to her and thanked her. What more did she want? Bea didn't know the answer, or, if she did, she wasn't ready to face it... With grim determination she got on with her work, and heaved a sigh of relief when it was time to go home.

Bea walked into her apartment. A long hot soak in the tub was what she needed. Half an hour later, she made herself a light meal and then settled down on the sofa, a glass of white wine on the table beside her. Too upset about Leon, she had made no arrangements to meet anyone so she had the whole weekend to herself.

Picking up the remote control, she switched on the television. Picking up the glass of wine, she took a sip— and then nearly choked. The glass slipped from her hand and bounced on the carpet, spraying her with wine. The seven o'clock news was on Channel Four, and there, standing with his arms around the shoulders of a tall, fair-headed European man on one side and an exquisitely beautiful Oriental girl on the other, was Leon. The news of his kidnap and subsequent release had broken, and he was being interviewed live on television.

Bea hardly heard the words; her whole attention was focused on Leon. He looked tired, and pale, and his magnificent black hair was cut close to his head.

'How did it feel to be locked in a cupboard, Mr Gregoris?' the interviewer asked.

Bea watched as Leon gave him a withering glance. 'Try it and see.'

The fair-headed man spoke up. 'Mr Gregoris has answered enough questions. He has been through a great ordeal, he is tired, and on his doctor's instructions he intends taking a few weeks' R and R. End of interview.'

It was strange seeing another man speaking for Leon, and even stranger that Leon had allowed him to. But seeing Leon finally put Bea's mind at rest, even if it was just on the television. Leaning forward, she picked up the glass from the floor, got up and headed for the kitchen. A glimmer of a smile tipped the corners of her full mouth but did not quite reach her eyes. Trust Leon; captured and shorn, he could still pull the most gorgeous female the very next day.

The following day, her apartment was clean, her washing done, and it was barely noon. Bea strolled into her bedroom, the rest of the weekend stretching before her as a total blank. She straightened the coverlet on the bed, not that it needed it, and wandered around aimlessly. She opened the wardrobe door. Yes! she decided on impulse, and half an hour later was dressed in her blue suit, *sans* blouse, but with the sapphire and diamond pendant Leon had given her for her birthday around her neck.

She left her apartment and hailed a cab. Settling in the back seat, she said to the driver, 'Knightsbridge, please.' She was going to act on Leon's advice and go on a shopping spree! Harrods and Harvey Nichols, here I come...

Five hours later, a tired but happy Bea stepped out of a cab about fifty yards from her building. The driver couldn't get any nearer because of the parked vehicles. She paid the fare and, after gathering a multitude of packages in both hands, turned to walk the last few yards home. She frowned; there seemed to be a crowd of people around the entrance, some kind of accident, fire or...

Before she could complete the thought, a voice yelled, 'There she is!' and she was surrounded by dozens of people. A microphone was stuck inches from her face, cameras flashed and she reeled back under the press of human bodies.

'Miss Stephen, the heiress?'

'Yes—no. I suppose so.' She was caught wide-eyed and stunned.

'How did you feel when Leon Gregoris was kidnapped?' 'Is it true you sanctioned the payment of the ransom?'

The questions flew fast and furious, and Bea was completely out of her depth. 'Upset, obviously. Yes. No.' She didn't know what to say. She had never had any dealings with the press or television before, and she was horrified. Clinging onto her shopping bags, she stumbled through one of the most embarrassing half-hours of her life. Eventually she managed to battle her way to the foyer of the building, where mercifully the security guard let her in and firmly refused entry to the media.

By the time she reached her apartment, reaction had set in. She collapsed on the sofa, shaking in every limb, her parcels discarded unnoticed on the floor. My God, she thought. Now she knew how Leon must feel. How on earth did he deal with the press so easily? They had turned her into a nervous wreck in a few minutes.

After a cup of sweet tea, and the relative silence of her home, she began to feel a little better. Well enough to unpack her purchases and put them away, and to begin to wonder how the media had found out who she was and where she lived.

She was still mulling over the problem when her doorbell rang. Bea automatically got up to open it, then stopped with her hand on the doorknob. What if a reporter had got into the building?

'Who is it?' she called, and smiled with relief at the sound of Margot's voice.

But her relief turned to squirming embarrassment as Margot dashed past her and switched on the television. 'You're famous, Bea.'

Bea looked at the picture with horrified eyes. There she was, in her blue suit, diamonds at her throat, loaded down with parcels from the top shops in town, and the commentator was calling her the 'Reluctant Heiress'. Then followed a sketchy history of her life and her business partnership with Leon Gregoris.

She didn't think it could get worse, but the Sunday papers the next morning were even more detailed, going so far as to print her address in Northumbria and a picture of her family home.

Margot was a tower of strength. 'Hey, Bea, as Andy Warhol said, it was your fifteen minutes of fame. Tomorrow someone else will be on the front page.'

And she was right. By Monday morning, when the two girls left for work, there was not a reporter in sight.

But as Bea walked into the office she began to realise the full extent of the damage caused by the press. Sophie, the receptionist, was the first.

'Good morning, Miss Stephen,' she said knowingly, and the rest of the staff followed suit.

Bea could see it in their eyes, the way they looked at her; a certain barrier was now in place. She was no longer Bea, the graduate trainee, but a person of power. By the end of the day she was forced to recognise that she was only comfortable around Tom Jordan and Margot.

Tuesday was even worse, but by Friday morning Bea was beginning to adjust to her new status. Leon was back in Cyprus, supposedly resting, but he rang Tom most days. Bea had spoken to him a few times and he seemed to be okay, if a bit abrupt. It was amazing how quickly things got back to normal, she mused.

Until Margot knocked on her apartment door and placed the daily paper in her hand.

'Sorry, Bea, some people just can't keep their mouths shut.'

'Why? What's happened?'

'Read the paper, take a look out of the window at the paparazzi, then decide if you want to go into the office.'

Bea rushed to the window. Margot was right; the reporters were back. Slowly she turned and crossed the room. She sank down onto the sofa and with growing horror read the newspaper article. It was full of sly innuendo that Leon and Bea were more than just business colleagues, that they were also lovers. An eye-witness account of Leon kissing Bea outside the office, which could only have been revealed by Sophie, the receptionist, seemed to confirm the fact. Also Andy, whom Bea had considered a friend, described her as 'a swinging girl who can't be pinned down'.

To cap it all, to Bea's utter amazement, some customer from the Muck and Money bar said he had seen Bea there with Leon and another man at the same time. Then he misquoted Leon's quip about bondage and kinky sex, making Bea out to be a cross between a sadomasochist and a *femme fatale*.

She did not go to work…

The next morning the ringing of the telephone woke her from a restless sleep. She groaned, and, reaching for the receiver, put it to her ear.

'Phoebe.'

It was Leon's voice, and she was struck by a sense of *déjà vu*. The last time he had awakened her with an early-morning call she had been suffering from a hangover. This time she simply felt tired and sadly disillusioned.

'What do you want?' she asked.

With a return to his old teasing ways, he answered, 'You, Phoebe.'

'Leon.' She said his name softly. 'It's good to know that after your ordeal you're still as incorrigible as ever.' He might be the biggest rake in the western world—what did she mean western world? He was as bad in the eastern world as well, it would seem!—but he was an old friend, and she felt as if she had very few left.

'No, I'm deadly serious. I've seen the newspaper reports and I know how much they must have upset you. Apparently my stepmother was interviewed in California and asked if she had put up the ransom. She gave them your name, but, in fairness to her, any serious reporter could easily have found out; it has never been a secret. However, I also know the media; they'll hound you to death until they get a statement. You can face them on your own, if you want to. But I have arranged to take care of it, if you're agreeable.'

'How?' she asked cautiously.

'I'll explain when I get there; expect me in twenty minutes.'

'You're in London?'

'Yes, and don't answer the door to anyone but me. Right?'

CHAPTER SEVEN

BEA slid out of bed and glanced from the telephone still in her hand to the blue sky outside, and then carefully replaced the receiver. She didn't have much choice. 'Damn the man,' she muttered.

Typical Leon; he had hung up on her before she'd had a chance to respond. She grimaced at the sight of the reporters already gathering on the pavement. Still, she reasoned, if Leon had a plan that would get her out of her apartment without having to run the gauntlet of the press hounds, it had to be worth considering.

The telephone shattered the silence. 'Hello, Leon,' she said, assuming it must be him calling back.

'Interesting! But no, Miss Stephen. This is Doug Brown, from the *Sunday Herald*.

At the mention of that particular tabloid newspaper Bea exploded. 'What? How did you get this number? It's ex-directory.'

She had thought at least she was protected from reporters telephoning her. She didn't wait to hear the man's answer but slammed the phone down, and, bending, unplugged it from the wall. Swiftly she dressed, then paced around her apartment, anger boiling within her. She felt like a caged animal, and suddenly she decided that anything Leon could come up with was all right by her. She had to get out or go mad...

By the time the doorbell rang Bea had calmed down somewhat, but she still felt like a fugitive in her own home. She whispered, 'Is that you, Leon?' When she heard his voice she opened the door, grabbed him by the arm and pulled him inside. 'Quick, someone might see you.'

'Don't be ridiculous, Phoebe; you sound like Inspector Clouseau on a bad day.' He walked along the short hall and into the living room, with Bea padding after him.

'Well, you never know,' she muttered defensively.

'With you, no,' Leon drawled sardonically, and, turning in the middle of the room, he flicked an unreadable glance over her. 'I did have to pass the press to get here, or did you imagine I was going to shin up a drainpipe, or lower myself in through a window off the roof?'

Leon could always be depended upon to make her feel like a fool. She reddened, because actually she *had* thought he would sneak in. 'Cut out the sarcasm and tell me this plan of yours. They have my telephone number now, though heaven knows how.'

She studied his darkly handsome face from beneath the veil of her lashes. The kidnap had taken its toll. His once long hair was now short, with the hint of a curl, and yet, if anything, it made him look even more attractive; he had a beautifully shaped head. But the lines had definitely deepened around his mouth and eyes. The ruthless strength and raw masculinity were evident as ever, but added to them was a coldly dispassionate cynicism, a world-weariness that the hero of her childhood, with his flowing ponytail and laughing eyes, would never have displayed.

She lowered her gaze down over his huge body. The elegant charcoal-grey suit hung not quite so perfectly on his tall frame. He had obviously lost weight, and suddenly her heart flooded with sympathy for him.

Acting on instinct, she crossed to where he stood in the middle of the room and wrapped her arms around him, her sole intention to give him a friendly hug. She tilted her head back to look up into his eyes.

'Sorry, Leon. Never mind my troubles. I should have asked. How are you coping?' Feeling the tension in his long body, and with a compassionate smile curling her mouth, she said softly, 'I really am sorry. I know it must have been terrible for you.'

Roughly he caught her upper arms and held her away from him, staring down at her with dark, almost angry eyes. 'Cut out the sympathy, Phoebe. I don't need your pity.'

So much for trying to comfort the man! she thought, feeling like a fool, and, shrugging off his hands, she stepped back. 'You're not going to get it,' she snapped. 'If it wasn't for you I wouldn't be in this mess.' Bea knew she was being unfair. Leon hadn't been able to help being kidnapped. But his curt dismissal of her offer of comfort had inexplicably hurt.

'I wondered how long it would take you to get around to blaming me,' Leon drawled cynically.

Bea took a deep breath, determined to hang onto her temper. After all, he had been through a harrowing ordeal. 'Look, Leon, let's not get into an argument.'

'You're right,' he said, and let his dark gaze sweep over her from head to toe, taking in her casual garb of old blue jeans and a red sweatshirt. 'First, get out of those clothes,' he added.

'What?' Her blue eyes widened in amazement. She hadn't let him into her flat to make a pass at her, but to rescue her.

'You can close your mouth, Phoebe. I promise I'm not going to seduce you. I simply want you dressed suitably. Put on that suit, the pendant and those shoes you were wearing in the newspaper photograph. The best form of defence is attack, so you and I will walk out of here together. I will make a short statement to the press that will satisfy them for the moment, but there's no reason to give them a different picture of you from the one they already have.'

She supposed it made sense. 'But then what?' she asked. It didn't seem much of a plan to her.

'Then you and I will take the company jet to Cyprus. I need a longer break, and a few days in the sun won't harm you, either. By the time you return to London, some other story will have hit the front page.'

'That's it? I go on holiday with you and hope the gossip blows over? I don't think so...' The thought of spending time alone with Leon on a Mediterranean island was all too seductive, and she doubted she would have the strength to resist him if he turned on his usual charm.

'Please yourself. If you want to face the press alone as the ''Reluctant Heiress'', as I believe they nicknamed you, or stay trapped in your apartment—fine. As a friend, I'm offering you a way out. But I'm leaving in ten minutes, with or without you. It makes no difference to me.'

'But—' She stopped. Her troubled gaze searched his face. He didn't seem concerned one way or the other, and the idea of a few days in Paphos was appealing. She hadn't been there long enough as a teenager to see anything, and he had said, 'as a friend'. But alone with Leon? Could she trust him? More importantly, could she trust herself?

'Before you ask, there are at least half a dozen staff at the villa. You won't be alone with me. And in any case I have work to catch up on. I promise you, flirtation is the last thing on my mind...'

She flushed slightly. How did he read her mind like that? 'I'll need time to pack,' she said, weakening.

'An overnight bag will do. I've told Tom Jordan you'll be away for a while, and I've arranged with Margot to pack your things and send them on. You'll have them by tomorrow night. So go and get changed and let's get out of here.'

Leon had thought of everything. And ten minutes later Bea learnt just what 'everything' entailed...

Leon slipped an arm around her waist as they exited the elevator on the ground floor. She tried to ease away—the warmth of his firm hand, even through the fabric of her jacket, had an unsettling effect on her already overstretched nerves—but Leon tightened his grip.

'Stick close to me, Phoebe, and let me do all the talking.' He slanted her a reassuring smile. 'Okay?'

She didn't have a lot of choice. They walked out of the front door and the flashing cameras blinded her. A dozen different voices yelled questions, so that Bea could hardly hear. She was glad of Leon's supporting arm, even if it did do funny things to her pulse rate. It was preferable to being pulled apart by what seemed like a pack of baying hounds.

When she did finally recover enough to make sense of what was being said, she got the shock of her life. She stared up at Leon in open-mouthed astonishment.

'Phoebe and I have been close for years. The pendant she is wearing was originally the betrothal ring I gave her when she was seventeen.' And with his free hand he lifted up the jewel while gazing like a besotted fool into Bea's upturned face.

'What?' she breathed stupidly. Surely no one could possibly believe such twaddle?

'I had it made into a necklace when we decided to wait until she had finished her studies before getting married. There's no longer any reason to delay. Phoebe and I are engaged and we are taking a short holiday in

South Africa, where Phoebe will choose her own uncut diamond and have it modelled exclusively for her as an engagement ring. I could do no less for my perfect bride.'

His captivity had clearly affected his brain. The man has gone mad, was Bea's first thought, and, tearing her gaze away from his, she looked down at the jewel he held between two long fingers. His knuckles brushed her throat, making her skin tingle, and she had difficulty concentrating. Originally she had only had the ring for less than twenty-four hours. Was it the same? she asked herself. And if so, why?

'Is that right, Miss Stephen? You and Mr Gregoris are to marry?' a reporter cried.

Then it hit her—why she had thought the pendant looked familiar when Leon had given it to her on her twenty-first. 'Yes, of course!' she exclaimed, finally recognising it. The gold ring was gone, and a slim gold base had been added, but it was the same. She shot a quizzical gaze up at Leon. What on earth did he think he was playing at?

'Wh—?' was as far as she got, before Leon's hard mouth descended over hers. His arms curved around her back, holding her firmly against his tall body while he kissed her with passionate possessiveness. She tried to resist. Eyes wide open, she caught the surprised but pleased faces of the crowd around them. Oh, no, she groaned inwardly, and then she was groaning aloud, for another reason, when Leon's tongue found entrance to the moist, sweet interior of her mouth.

Bea sagged when Leon finally broke the kiss, and only his arm around her waist stopped her from falling flat on her face. Before she could gather her scattered wits, Leon was pushing her into the back seat of a chauffeur-driven limousine and sliding in beside her.

The car was moving before Bea recovered her composure, and with it a rising tide of anger swelled in her breast. Face scarlet, her skirt halfway up her thighs, she turned her furious gaze upon Leon.

He was sitting beside her, one hand unfastening the tie at his throat and then the first couple of buttons of his shirt. He lounged back, his long legs stretched out in front of him, his jacket undone, apparently totally unconcerned by their recent hustle with the press.

He looked so damned satisfied, and in his rumpled state so infinitely attractive, that suddenly Bea saw red and exploded in a tirade of abuse.

'Are you stark staring mad, Leon? Has being kidnapped pickled your brain or something? Your plan was supposed to help me escape the press. Some plan! What on earth possessed you to tell that lot we were getting married? Tell the driver to turn the car around this minute, or I will. I'd rather be trapped in my apartment than trapped into an engagement to you.'

'And I have no desire to be trapped in an engagement to you.' Leon slanted her a cynical glance. 'But the strategy did work. The press are happy with their scoop, and we are free and clear.'

He made it sound so reasonable, yet Bea's feminine intuition was telling her there was something seriously wrong with Leon's scenario. He might have vastly more experience of the press than she did, but she was not a complete fool. 'I still think we should go back and tell the truth.'

The sardonic look he gave her made the colour surge in her cheeks. 'The truth?' he mocked. 'If you recall, my dear Phoebe, you were asked if my statement was true, and I, and the reporters present, distinctly heard you say, "Yes, of course!"'

She flung up her hands in a gesture of exasperation.

'But I meant I had recognised the pendant, not—not…'
She stumbled to a halt as Leon grasped the waving hand
nearest to him.

'Stop it—forget it. In a couple of weeks the gossip
will have blown over and we can go our own ways.'
Dropping her hand, Leon slouched back in his seat, effectively dismissing her objections.

'That's all very well for you,' she snapped. 'The press
are used to your licentious ways. But I'll never live it
down. They'll never leave me alone—or I'll be known
as the dumped fiancée of the great Leon Gregoris. My
God! I can't believe you.'

'You never did trust me,' Leon slashed back, brutally
but quietly. 'So just shut up, Phoebe, and do as you're
told.'

Leon had never spoken to her in such a ruthless man-
ner before and it stopped her cold. She searched his
harshly set features suspiciously. She didn't know this
man at all; his dark eyes evaded her gaze and instead he
looked out of the window.

She took a deep breath. 'The plan was a short holiday
in Paphos; are we still going there, not to deepest
Africa?' she demanded scathingly. She needed some
clarification from Leon, some sign to allay her mounting
disquiet at the situation.

'Yes, of course. The rest was a false trail for the benefit of the press.'

'Humph, some trail,' she snapped, still riled by his
stupid engagement story. It was all right for him, he was
a notorious womaniser, but when the truth came out she
would look like another one of his pitiful cast-offs.

'Drop it,' Leon said harshly, but she noticed he still
avoided looking at her.

The rest of the journey was conducted in almost complete silence. Bea, simmering with resentment at the

false position Leon had engineered, glanced around the interior of the car. It was luxury personified. A glass partition separated the chauffeur from the occupants— all very private. As for her companion, he had the smug, self-satisfied look of a man in total control. Her resent- ment bubbled over into sarcasm.

'The limousine is quite a change for you, Leon. I never thought I would see the day when the great Leon Gregoris would allow someone else to drive him.'

'I learn by my mistakes.' Leon swung around, and the embittered black eyes that met hers sent an icy shiver down her spine. 'In Hong Kong I stopped for petrol. While I was paying for it the bastards hid on the back seat. Never again.'

'Your one indulgence is your cars,' she said softly, horrified by the brief glimpse she had seen of the kidnap and how it had affected him.

'Not any more,' he said flatly, and returned his atten- tion to the view from the window.

The flight to Cyprus was not much better, though Bea had never been on a private jet before. She looked around in awe at the thick-pile carpet, the soft cream hide chairs and sofa and the heavy glass table bolted to the floor, plus an extensively equipped bar in one corner.

'You certainly know how to live, Leon,' she quipped.

Black-lashed glittering eyes met hers in a challenging glance. 'This is also yours, Phoebe. Do *you* know how to live?' he demanded mockingly.

Bea retreated to the safety of a seat at the back of the cabin without answering. Reluctantly she fastened her seat belt, wondering if she was doing the right thing. There was something different about Leon. She couldn't put her finger on it.

She chewed her bottom lip nervously as the roar of the plane engine signalled take-off. It was too late to escape now, she thought, and then wondered why the word 'escape' had entered her mind. She was getting fanciful, she told herself firmly. This was a brief holiday in the sun, with a family friend, in a house full of staff. It would be a breeze, and then back to London and work.

She was still telling herself the same story when she stepped out of the aircraft at Paphos airport, the warmth of the late October sun lifting her spirits and her confidence. Another limousine was waiting, and it drove them through the countryside and up the twisting mountain road that led to the villa.

Her first shock was the twelve-foot-high iron gates, and the armed security guard on duty. 'Leon.' She swivelled round in her seat. He'd had his head stuck in papers from his briefcase virtually since leaving London. He looked up and out of the window.

'Good. We've arrived.'

'Yes, but I don't remember iron gates and a guard.' She looked around her, her eyes widening in puzzlement. The white perimeter wall was still there, but now it was topped with what looked suspiciously like six feet of electric fencing.

'Yes, well, more trouble surged up between the Turkish and Greek sectors not so long ago, and I decided on a little more security. As it turns out, it was lucky I did.'

She stared at him warily. 'Lucky? Surely the fighting wasn't that bad?' She had seen something on the news, but it had sounded more like an unfortunate skirmish than anything major.

'Forget it, Phoebe. Welcome to my home.'

The car slipped slowly between the massive gates after the security guard had carefully checked the driver and the occupants of the car.

'Fort Knox springs to mind,' she tried to joke, but Leon did not share her humour.

'It is necessary,' he replied bluntly.

The limousine came to a halt before white marble steps that led to massive double entrance doors forged in bronze.

The staff had emerged to greet them, and as Bea stepped out of the car she smiled in recognition at the old housekeeper and her husband, Anna and Spiros. She had met them on her last brief visit. The dark-eyed young maids were all strangers but Leon, taking her arm, duly introduced Bea to everyone as they walked up the steps.

The two burly men at the top guarding the door she could have done without knowing, Bea thought as Leon guided her into the shadowed coolness of the wide reception hall.

'I'll show you to your room.' He glanced at his wristwatch. 'You have exactly fifteen minutes to settle in. Anna insists on serving an English tea out on the patio at four.'

'That's sweet,' Bea said with a smile, and her smile broadened considerably when Leon ushered her into what was to be her room for the holiday.

At least he'd had the sensitivity not to put her in the same room as last time, and for that she was grateful. Plus, if memory served her right, this huge, elegant room had been his stepmother's room before, and it was at the opposite end of the villa to his room.

Why the distance should make her feel safe she did not query. Instead she turned smiling eyes to Leon. 'Thank you, it's a gorgeous room.'

One dark brow rose sardonically. 'Don't thank me, thank Anna; it was her idea. She's trying to impress you.

She never quite got over your hasty departure last time. Hence the tea and the master suite.'

'I will,' she murmured as he left.

A brief exploration of the room revealed a door leading to a dressing room lined with wardrobes and an ultra-modern functional dressing table. A further door opened into a luxurious bathroom.

She looked longingly at the spa bath, but, mindful of tea in fifteen minutes, she contented herself with washing her face and hands and running a comb through her long hair. Finding her way back downstairs, she consoled herself with the thought that she couldn't have got changed anyway; all she had in her holdall was a change of underwear, a nightshirt and her toiletries.

Anna had really gone to town for the tea. Bea smiled as she walked down the steps from the main living room onto the patio. A wrought-iron table was covered in a white damask cloth, and two places were set with delicately patterned bone-china cups and plates. A silver cakestand took centre-stage, loaded with a variety of delicious-looking, fat-making cakes. Three more plates stacked with finger sandwiches, and a plate of scones, completed the picture. Bea had barely sat down when Anna arrived, carrying a silver tea service on an elegant matching tray.

Leon reappeared as she drained her second cup of tea, having eaten two cakes too many. 'What kept you?' she demanded huskily. Poor Anna had apologised over and over again for his absence, but it was not that so much as the way he looked that affected her tone of voice.

Her wide blue eyes took in his appearance, from the sheen of dampness on his short black curling hair—obviously he had showered—down to his broad shoulders. The suit had been replaced by a plain black polo shirt that moulded his muscular chest and revealed his tanned forearms. Well-worn black jeans and a leather belt with an intricately designed brass buckle to support them hung low on his lean hips. He looked dark and dangerous, and a frisson of warning slid down her spine as he came towards her and stopped, towering over her.

'Well?' she prompted—anything to break the lengthening silence.

He studied her long blonde hair, which a slight breeze had tousled into tumbling disarray around her beautiful face, and the tight clasp of her fingers on the delicate handle of the bone-china cup. He took his time looking her over, a glitter of gold brightening his black eyes. A brilliant smile curved his sensuous mouth, making her aware of the virile sensuality he exuded without even trying. 'What kept me?' he echoed throatily. 'If I had known you missed me I would have been here like a shot.'

'I didn't miss you. I just…' She ground to a halt at his mocking laugh.

'Same old Phoebe. You certainly know how to make a man feel good,' he drawled, and, reaching down, caught hold of her hand. 'Come on, I'll show you around before the sun goes down. There have been quite a few changes since the last time you were here.'

She got to her feet and for the next half-hour she duly admired the new extension. By the time Leon led her out into the garden and insisted they watch the sunset she was almost relaxed in his company—until he put his arm around her shoulders.

Bea stiffened instinctively. They were alone on the terrace, their vantage point for watching the sunset. She tried to ease away from the disturbing warmth of his large frame, but he simply tightened his hold.

'The days are still hot in October, but at this time in

the evening the air cools rapidly, and you have no other protection but me. So be still, Phoebe, and watch.'

The sunset was magnificent, and she sighed with pleasure as together they watched the fiery red ball sink into the sea far away to the right.

'Worth the wait, but then the best things in life are,' Leon offered softly, turning her back towards the house.

She glanced up at him; it was hard to see his expression in the dim light, and for a second she thought she saw a gleam of triumph in his dark eyes. But once back inside she knew she was mistaken.

His arm falling from her shoulders, Leon smiled blandly down at her. 'Sorry, I have to leave you to your own devices until dinner at nine. I have work to do.' And again he walked away.

Once more in her bedroom, Bea kicked off her shoes and padded across to the bathroom. She turned on the taps of the spa bath, and, spying a collection of toiletries, chose a bottle of bath crystals and tipped half into the swirling water. Over the sound of the running water she heard someone knock on the bedroom door. Padding back through the bedroom, she went to open it and found Anna.

'Miss Phoebe, you like I press your clothes? The master say your luggage not yet arrived.'

'Thanks, that's a great idea. Come in.' In seconds Bea had stripped off her jacket and skirt and handed them to Anna. 'Just come in when you're finished. I'm going to wallow in the bath.'

Back in the bathroom she slid off her bra and briefs. As she bent to turn off the taps the gold chain around her throat fell forward. Her eye caught the pendant and she frowned. Turning off the water, she straightened up and removed the jewel, then she turned it over slowly in her small hand.

Walking back into the dressing room, she let the gold chain trickle through her fingers. Leon had told the truth: it was the original ill-fated ring. Strange that he should have bothered to have it altered. He could just as easily have passed it on to one of his many ladyfriends. No— he was far too cagey a bachelor for that, she realised. He would never give a mistress a ring. She might get the wrong idea!

Still, it was odd. Leon was a generous man; he could easily have bought her something new for her birthday. So why this? She picked up her bag from the dresser and slipped the pendant in the interior pocket. Whatever his reason, she was not going to wear it again; it made her uneasy somehow...

Half an hour later, feeling relaxed and refreshed, Bea stepped out of the bath and, wrapping a large towel around her wet body, swiftly washed her bra and pants in the vanity basin and hung them on the towel rail to dry. She was smiling to herself as she walked back into the dressing room; somehow, wet underwear hanging around looked oddly out of place in the luxurious bathroom.

She rummaged in her holdall for the spare set she had packed and, finding them, dried herself thoroughly and slipped on the matching white lace briefs and bra. Sitting at the dressing table, she quickly blow-dried her long hair, curving it under like a page boy's with the help of a hairbrush. Satisfied with the result, she applied the minimum of make-up: a moisturiser—her skin needed nothing more—a quick flick of the mascara wand to accentuate her long lashes, a touch of pink lipstick and she was almost ready.

Back in the bedroom, she looked around for her clothes just as Anna, after a brief knock, walked in.

'Thank you, Anna.' She took the garments with a smile and slipped on the skirt.

'It is my pleasure. For many years we have waited for your return. It is not good for the master to be alone.' Her eyes rested benignly on Bea's face. 'But now you are here to stay and everything is right again.'

'For a holiday,' Bea said awkwardly, not quite knowing what to say. The poor woman had obviously got the wrong end of the stick somehow. But it wasn't up to Bea to disillusion her; she would leave that to Leon, after she had left.

Slipping on her jacket, she strolled across to the French windows. Opening them, she stepped out onto the balcony. Taking a few deep breaths, she savoured the clear night air. It was a beautiful spot.

Best of all, there was not a reporter or photographer in sight... The pressure of the last few days and weeks fell away and she felt rejuvenated. Leon's plan wasn't all that bad, she conceded.

She looked around in pleasure at the beauty of the night, and then she stiffened. The serpent in Eden! she thought with a grim smile as her gaze caught the moonlight glinting on metal, and a man patrolling the wall with a gun.

Abruptly she turned. Finding her shoes, she slipped them on and left the room. After one or two false moves Bea found the dining room. It was an elegant room, overlooking the bay, and had an enormous table with seating for twelve. Standing by the window was Leon.

'Do we have to eat in here?' she blurted, disturbed by the sight of Leon in a white dinner jacket, a vivid reminder of the last time she had been in this room with him. 'And aren't you a tad overdressed?' she opined, suddenly no longer relaxed. Instead she could feel the tension simmering in the air between them. Was Leon remembering that last time, when she had broken their engagement? Had he dressed exactly the same again as a taunting reminder?

'I told you, Anna is insisting on doing everything correctly, and I wouldn't dare argue with her,' he responded, with an amused lift of his eyebrow, and, crossing to the table, he pulled out a chair to the right of the one at the head and indicated that she should sit down.

Studying his face, Bea was not convinced his reason was so simple. She had not forgotten his lie to the press that they were once again engaged. She couldn't put her finger on it, but she sensed something sinister lurking beneath his bland expression.

'That reminds me,' she said, sitting down and shaking out her napkin. She placed it on her lap before glancing up at Leon, who had taken his own seat at the head of the table. 'Anna seems to have some weird idea I'm staying here for a lot longer than a few days.'

'Have some wine and relax; you're imagining things.' He filled a crystal glass with sparkling wine and offered it to her.

She took it, and their fingers touched with a sudden tingle of awareness that made her pulse flutter. Hastily she took a gulp of the wine. She hadn't imagined his effect on her, and whispered under her breath, 'Oh, Lord, don't let him get to me.' But it was a futile prayer.

Anna served the meal—a mixed fish platter, which Bea found very appetizing, followed by roast lamb with an assortment of herbs, which gave it a tangy flavour. But halfway through Bea found her appetite dwindling.

Leon kept her glass topped up with wine and made pleasant, uncontroversial conversation. But she just couldn't relax. The silences between them grew longer. She found her eyes straying to his mobile mouth, found

herself gulping as he unselfconsciously licked his lips.
He sounded amiable enough, but she could not dismiss
the feeling that underneath he was watching her with a
brooding intensity that was not in the least amiable.

When he suggested they have their coffee in the main
lounge, she jumped out of her seat before he could help
her.

'If you don't mind, I'll give the coffee a miss. I think
I'll just go to bed.'

'So soon?' Leon queried, and she flushed as she saw
the sardonic gleam in his dark eyes.

'Well, with the press and everything, I haven't had
much sleep the past few nights, and coffee keeps me
awake,' she returned quickly, backing towards the door.

'Then of course you must go to bed. I'll see you to
your room.'

'No, really.'

'I insist.'

Bea mounted the staircase with Leon a step behind
her. She was sure she could feel his hot breath on the
back of her neck, and she asked herself how she could
have been so stupid as to get herself in this position.
Turning at the door to her room to say goodnight and
goodbye, she found her face only inches from his chest.
Her head shot back and she put her hands on his chest
to ward him off.

'Are you frightened of me, sweet Phoebe?' Leon
drawled silkily, capturing her hands on his chest in one
of his much larger ones.

'No, no, of course not.' But she lied. His black eyes
burned down into hers and she recognised the glint of
desire—and something else she couldn't name.

'Then why are you looking at me like a startled rabbit?' he demanded mockingly.

'I'm not,' she squeaked.

'Good.' With his free hand he opened the bedroom door and backed her inside.

'Goodnight, Leon.' She forced his name past her stiff lips, suddenly more afraid than she had ever been in her life, and hoping he would just go.

'One kiss, and then—'

'Please, you're being silly, Leon.' She cut him off, but stood frozen to the spot, caught between fear and fascination as he let go of her hands. In one deft movement he had undone her jacket and slid it from her shoulders to lie at her feet. His smouldering glance fell to the full curves of her breasts, cupped in a wisp of white lace.

'What do you think you're playing at?' she snapped belatedly, and felt the colour surge to her face even as she crossed her arms defensively over her chest. 'Don't be a fool, Leon. You promised.' She tried to reason with him, displaying a cool sophistication she was far from feeling. 'Friends, remember? No seduction.' Seemingly casually, she bent to retrieve her jacket.

His hand snaked out and fastened around her arm. 'No, once before I was a fool. I was stupid enough to leave you at the bedroom door. But never again.' Pulling her against him, and with his other hand lacing up into her trailing hair, he gently tugged her head back to expose her throat.

'No, no, you can't!' she cried, losing her cool. But his face became a blur as he lowered his head, and his lips trailed kisses of fire across the curve of her breast, up her throat, before his hard mouth captured hers.

CHAPTER EIGHT

IT ALL happened so quickly; one minute Bea was outside her room, the next she was inside, naked to the waist apart from a wisp of lace, and crushed against Leon's powerful body.

All thought of remaining sophisticated fled from her mind under the demanding pressure of his lips. Bea, hands flailing wildly, lashed out at any part of him she could reach in an effort to break free. But his mouth ravaged hers, and the all-consuming passion of his kiss evoked a response that insidiously drained her resistance.

'Tonight you're mine,' he growled against her lips, breaking the kiss to trail a string of kisses back down her throat. He stopped where the pulse beat madly in her neck and sucked on the tender flesh.

Her heart beating frantically, her breasts pressing painfully against the restrictive white lace of her bra, Bea groaned, 'No-o-o.'

He swallowed her denial with his mouth and swung her up in his arms. He carried her across the room and lowered her onto the bed. His mouth never left hers as he snapped on the bedside light, illuminating the room in an intimate golden glow.

When he finally released her, she found herself staring breathlessly up into the night-black darkness of Leon's eyes, and what she saw made her come alive to what was happening. Pure panic made her renew her efforts to escape. She struggled to sit up, but with one large hand he pressed her back down, and, with a dexterity born of vast experience, he shrugged out of his jacket and shirt.

'Stop it, Leon. You can't...' she cried, even as her mouth dried at the sight of his muscular bronzed chest, its dark covering of soft hair arrowing down to disappear beneath the waistband of his trousers. Trousers he was deftly unfastening, her mesmerised gaze discovered!

'I can,' he grated. 'I want you, and you can lie through your teeth denying it, but your body tells a different story.' His glittering gaze skimmed over the curves of her breasts as his trousers hit the floor, and he slid onto the bed, turning his powerful naked body towards her, partially blocking out the light and shadowing his handsome features.

His dark eyes bored into hers as she lay paralysed by a reluctant fascination. His strong arms at either side of her slender body caged her, and the weight of one long, muscular leg, thrown over hers, pinned her to the bed.

'You... Leon... You don't mean it. You'll hate yourself,' she babbled, hoping to deflect him from the avowed intent she read in his narrowed eyes. This was a Leon she didn't recognise: cold and determined. Gone was the easygoing, charming companion, and in his place was a man she instinctively knew would not take no for an answer.

'Leon, please...' She tried again as his long fingers deftly unclipped her bra and threw it to one side.

'Oh, I am going to please you, sweet Phoebe.' His hand stroked across her full breasts, his thumb casually grazing the rosy peaks. 'See how you respond?' His dark eyes lingered on her naked breasts, and a slow, sensuous smile curved his hard mouth as the rosy peaks hardened beneath his fingers.

A shaft of arrowing excitement shuddered through her as his hand moved expertly against her breast, cupping and stroking, rolling the sensitised peak between his fingers. She was helpless against his sexual onslaught, and a low moan escaped her.

'I tried to do the correct thing once. I let you tease me for years. But no more,' he grated, his hand stroking down to her waist.

Through a sensuous haze she heard his words. Had she teased him? Her confused mind tried to find the answer. But his clever, caressing hands robbed her of the power to think straight.

'I was a fool. I could have had you but I wanted more.'

Yes, that was the trouble. Her dulled mind suddenly cleared. The swine had wanted more. One woman was never enough for him; he wanted hundreds. The thought renewed her resolve to fight him off, and she lashed out with her fist. He caught her wrist and held it over her head, his glittering gaze raking her flushed face.

'Stop fighting me, Phoebe. I am nothing like the young boys you're used to. What did your friend tell the press?' he queried savagely. '"A swinging girl who can't be pinned down."'

'Andy did—'

'I don't want to hear what any other man did to you. I've ached for years, and tonight you are going to feel just some of what I have suffered, before finding pleasure you have never dreamed of with your young boys,' he drawled arrogantly.

Pinned beneath him, with the heat of his body enveloping her, it was hard to think straight, but she realised Leon actually thought she was experienced.

'No, Leon, you don't under—' She never finished.

Leon muttered something thickly in Greek and smothered her mouth with his, kissing her with devouring hunger. His hand stroked back up to cup her breast, then he grazed his lips down her throat until his mouth covered her hard nipple, and then with tongue and teeth he stroked and bit in an exquisite tormenting caress, while his fingers found her other breast and teased with subtle expertise.

The blood pounded through her veins, sheer pleasure lancing through her body, and she whimpered with delight. The rest of her clothes were removed without Bea even realising it until Leon knelt up on the bed, his arm curving around her back as he lifted her up towards him.

'You liked that, Phoebe,' he rasped, and kissed the tip of each breast before holding her a little away from him. 'Let me look at you, Phoebe.' His black eyes, lit with the flame of desire, studied her naked body. 'You are so beautiful. Your skin is as pale and as fine as a moth's wing. I can almost see your heart fluttering in your chest.'

Bea, her sensually drugged gaze slowly focusing, swallowed hard, and almost choked as she experienced a feeling more earthy. She had never seen a totally nude man in the flesh before, and Leon was magnificent. The light played across his broad shoulders and down over his flat belly to where the source of his manhood stood proud and erect. It was vaguely frightening. He was like a statue of a Greek god, perfect in feature and form, but very much alive, with the dark, domineering strength of a man who was supremely confident in his mastery of the female sex.

What was she doing here? Naked on a bed with Leon? Her worst nightmare! Or was it her ultimate fantasy? a tiny devil whispered in her brain. Panicking, she grabbed his shoulders and tried to push him away, but he simply slipped his hands around her waist and lowered his head

to hers, and the force of his kiss drove her back down
onto the mattress, his long body following.

The power of his kiss inflamed her senses, and the
feel of his naked body moving smoothly against hers,
flesh on flesh, was like being stroked by satin and steel.
But still she made one last effort to deter him. She dug
her fingernails into his shoulders. 'Don't do this, Leon.'

He looked down at her hectically flushed face, his
black eyes glittering with gold. He moved against her
again, then his hand stroked down over her stomach and
slid between her legs, his palm cupping her feminine
mound.

She gasped as his long fingers delved into the hot, wet
warmth, and she shuddered uncontrollably.

'But you want me to...' Leon rasped throatily.

She was drowning in a sensuous world of physical
pleasure. One finger pressed on the nub of her feminine
joy. Her thighs parted slightly and she bit back a moan.

'Badly...' Leon growled. His eyes, brilliant with triumph, burned into hers, and deliberately he bent his head
and licked the taut peak of one breast while his seeking
fingers continued their devilish torment. This time she
could not hold back the moan. Her hands snaked around
the nape of his neck, and she was lost.

'Desperately,' he added roughly, capturing her swollen lips again in a passionate, teasing kiss.

Bea could not deny him. Her lips parted and welcomed the thrusting invasion of his tongue. Her small
hands urgently roamed over the muscle and sinew of his
broad back and she cried out when once again his mouth
found her breast.

All the while his long, sensitive fingers explored her
intimately, until she was a writhing mass of burning sensation. Muscles she'd never known she had were clenching and unclenching in aching, desperate need. Perspira-

tion dampened her skin; her eyes lost their focus. She was aware of nothing but Leon, his strength and power, and the promise of pleasure unimaginable.

Only slowly did she realise he had stopped, that most of his weight had lifted from her.

'Open your eyes and say it,' Leon ground out between clenched teeth. 'Look at me.'

Slowly she opened her eyes and met his brilliant black gaze.

'Tell me what you want, Phoebe,' he demanded harshly.

She could not have denied him to save her life. 'You,' she breathed, and for a brief second wondered what else she had to tell him. But, reaching her small hands up to tangle in the soft hair of his chest and, more bravely, to stroke down to cup the core of his masculinity, she forgot everything.

His mighty frame shuddered. 'At last,' he groaned, and bestowed a kiss of infinite possession on her swollen lips.

Her legs parted wider to welcome him and his large hands cupped her buttocks, lifting her from the bed. He took her in a sudden mighty thrust.

Bea screamed, but her cry of pain was stifled moments later beneath Leon's lips as he stilled inside her.

'Hush, Phoebe. I did not know,' he murmured against her mouth.

'No... Please,' she begged, her body taut with the unexpected pain.

'Yes.' His lips brushed against her ear, sending a little shiver through her which intensified when he slowly withdrew, then eased gently back inside her. 'Trust me, Phoebe. Relax.' His deep, rough voice murmured comfort and encouragement. His hands moved to stroke the length of her legs. He continued to caress her, stroking her breasts, her stomach and the place where they were still joined.

Bea forgot the pain, forgot everything but the heady sensual emotions Leon was arousing in her. And, sensing her receptiveness, Leon thrust deeper. Bea's body arched convulsively, the pleasure so intense that she cried out again, but this time in ecstasy. She clung to him, her untutored body quickly adjusting to the rhythm he set. Wave after wave of indescribable sensation sent her shuddering to the edge, and she heard Leon's triumphant cry as his life force exploded inside her and she went careening over the edge, consumed by the fire of fulfillment into a moment of complete oblivion.

From a long way off she heard Leon's voice and opened her eyes. She was conscious of nothing except the thudding of her heart—or was it his?—and Leon's long body stretched out beside her. So that was what it was all about, she thought in awe. A rapturous feeling of complete union between two people, at one in body and soul.

'Phoebe?' Leon raised himself up on one elbow and frowned down at her. 'Are you all right?'

'Mmm,' she murmured, lazily studying him. His black hair was flat to his head with sweat, and beads of moisture glistened on his curling chest hair. She reached up a finger to trace around the sensuous line of his mouth. He had a wonderful mouth. But he caught her hand and pushed it away.

'Why didn't you tell me you were still a virgin?'

'Does it matter?' she sighed, wallowing in the glorious afterglow of loving.

'Not to me. Not now.' And, lowering his lips briefly to her breast, where her nipple instantly responded to his touch, he grinned in satisfaction and drawled mockingly, 'In fact I can almost feel sorry for Andy and the rest.'

Collapsing back on the bed, his hands behind his head, he added, 'Obviously you were a touch-but-don't-take tease. A type I always avoided in the past. But not any more; you were quite a revelation, Phoebe.'

His reference to her sexuality and supposed past boyfriends brought her down to earth with a thud. No tender words of love or reassurance... The greatest moment in her life, and for Leon she was nothing but another lay. What had she done? Her emotions raw, tears welled up in her eyes, but she blinked them back. She would not give him the satisfaction of knowing he had hurt her.

Sitting up, she found the sheet and drew it up to hide her nakedness. He had even left the light on, and somehow that only seemed to add to her shame and humiliation. How could she have given everything to this man? The one man she had vowed not to get involved with.

She turned her head and glanced down at Leon. He was lying there, a perfect picture of the satiated male, with about as much sensitivity as a brick wall...

She had not the strength to be angry; instead a blessed numbness enveloped her and, with what little self-esteem she had left, she forced herself to speak.

'Yes, well, if you say so. Who am I to argue with a man of your vast experience? But would you please leave? I want to sleep.' Her decision was made in an instant. She was leaving tomorrow—getting off this island and out of his life. She would rather face the world press than end up as another one of Leon's playthings.

Bea brushed the hair back from her forehead with a shaky hand, wondering how she could have been so foolish as to imagine they had shared an almost mystical experience. Two people joined in body and soul! Leon had long since lost count of the women who had shared his bed. As for his soul, she doubted he had one...

Slowly, Leon sat up. Naked and unashamed, he turned

his dark gaze on her pale face. 'What the hell are you talking about?' he said, with a softness that was more threatening than shouting. 'You belong to me, and we share a bed.'

'No,' Bea said firmly. 'It was an interesting experience, and you can mark another notch on your belt. You got what you wanted. Now go.'

His dark eyes flared with anger. 'No way,' he snapped. The light went out at the touch of his hand, and the room was plunged into darkness.

Bea could make out his large shape and felt his hand tug the sheet from her grasp. 'What are you doing?'

'Expanding your education, Phoebe. Obviously you know very little about men if you imagine once is enough,' Leon's deep voice drawled silkily. He ran a taunting hand down over her breasts. 'That was for starters, if you like. The main course is the fun.'

His lips touched hers, and to her never-ending shame she was too weak to resist. Or maybe a tiny part of her brain said, Why not? She was leaving tomorrow. Who could begrudge her one night of passion? It might be the only passion she would ever know.

That thought scared her more than anything. It was tantamount to admitting Leon was the only man for her... She closed her eyes tight and gave herself up to the pleasure of his kiss, and within moments she was drowning in a sea of sensuous delight...

Bea opened her eyes. Dazzling sunlight made her blink sleepily, and the delicious smell of fresh coffee teased her nostrils. She tried to sit up and it was then she realised that a very masculine tanned arm, lightly dusted with black hair, was clamped firmly around her waist. Please let me be dreaming, she prayed, but she turned her head slightly and her gaze fell upon the sleeping face of Leon. 'Oh, God!' she groaned.

'Good morning.'

It got worse... Anna appeared at the side of the bed with a tray loaded with two cups and saucers, coffee jug, cream and sugar.

'Anna,' Bea murmured weakly, and, carefully lifting Leon's arm from her waist, she sat up. 'I...you...' Her face turning scarlet with embarrassment, she battled on, 'It's not what...'

'Shh, I understand,' Anna said in a whisper, a broad smile lighting her plump face, and, placing the tray on the bedside table, she added, 'We no wake the master. It is long time since he sleep.'

With the events of last night giving an instant replay in her mind, Bea's blush deepened even further. Trust the pig to sleep on, she thought bitterly. Again and again in the night he had turned to her, and she had been putty in his hands. Now she had to face Anna, stricken with guilt and embarrassment, while he snored. He had no conscience. But then she had always known that.

'Thank you, Anna.' Casting a glance around the room, she spied her scattered clothes. 'Would you mind pressing my suit again?' she asked. It was all she had to wear, and she wanted to get out of here as quickly as possible.

'No need, Anna.' Leon sat up, very much awake. Curving an arm around Bea's waist, he nuzzled her neck, the morning stubble on his jaw grazing her skin. 'Phoebe, darling, we can stay here till your luggage arrives, or there are some clothes my stepmother left in the wardrobe. Take your pick. But I know which I prefer,' he drawled throatily.

Anna, beaming benignly on what she perceived as the happy couple, scooted out of the room. Bea, with a hard fist to Leon's chest that sent him sprawling back on the pillows, scooted out of bed. Grabbing the sheet and wrapping it around her naked body, she let her gaze skim the tray. Two cups. *Two* cups! And then it clicked.

She spun around, the full fury of her blue eyes blasting the man reclining stark naked on the bed. 'Two cups... You planned all this. You even told Anna,' she spluttered in her rage. 'It's one thing to be seduced on the spur of the moment, but, but...' Words failed her.

'Seduced? You? You couldn't get enough,' Leon responded with a shout of laughter. Bea dashed to the dressing room and into the bathroom, his mocking laughter ringing in her ears.

She locked the door behind her and, dropping the sheet, entered the shower and turned on the water, before giving way to tears of hurt, anger and bitter humiliation.

He was right. She had acted like a woman possessed. She had gloried in his lovemaking, had willingly followed him down the paths of erotic delight that he, with his vast experience, had revealed to her. The unfamiliar aches and a light bruise on her naked body bore testimony to the fact, she sadly admitted to herself as she scrubbed and rubbed her naked flesh in an attempt to wash away his touch.

But never again, she silently vowed. After removing the lingerie she had left to dry on the towel rail the night before and slipping it on, she unlocked the bathroom door and entered the dressing room. Fearful that at any moment Leon might burst in, she hastily searched the wardrobes. Finding a pair of plain black chinos, she pulled them on; they were a bit tight, but would do. A skimpy white knit cropped top completed the ensemble. With her long hair still damp, and stuck behind her ears, she straightened her spine and, picking up her bag from the dresser, marched back into the bedroom, expecting to face her Nemesis.

The room was empty, the bed made afresh—no sign of her night of debauchery, or of Leon. Bea breathed a sigh of relief and, spying her blue high-heeled pumps, slipped them on her feet. Hardly haute couture, if the press were waiting when she arrived back in London, she thought grimly. But what the hell? So long as she got away from Leon.

The kitchen was empty, much to Bea's relief, and, crossing to where the telephone was fixed to the wall, she picked it up. Ten minutes later, she slammed it back down in exasperation. It had been easy enough to get through to the British Airways office—most Greek Cypriots spoke some English, probably because the British armed forces had been a presence on the island for decades—but, unfortunately, the earliest she could get a seat on a flight back to London was tomorrow.

Worrying her bottom lip with her teeth, Bea moved around the kitchen, making her breakfast. Anna was probably at the vegetable market. Finally, she sat down at the kitchen table and pondered her dilemma.

By the time she had finished eating, a kernel of an idea had taken root in her mind, and, draining the last of her coffee, she stood up with a determined expression on her face. Leaving the kitchen, she headed for the study.

Taking a deep breath, she opened the door and walked in. Leon was sitting behind a large leather-topped desk, his dark head bent over some papers. He looked up at her arrival, the beginnings of a smile curving his sexy mouth.

'Good. You have recovered from your sulks, Phoebe?' Rising to his feet, he strolled towards her. 'It is not unusual after a girl's first time for her to feel upset—angry, even. But—'

'But nothing,' she cut in, astounded by his arrogant

complacency. Her eyes took in his large form, casually dressed in blue jeans and a blue denim shirt; he looked disgustingly, vibrantly male. His hand reached out to her shoulder, but, hanging onto her anger, she shrugged it off, moving around him. 'I want to contact the company jet.' She swung on her heel to face him again. 'I am leaving. Today.'

'Are you, now?' Leon drawled softly, closing the door and leaning back against it.

'Yes,' she said curtly. 'As you have reminded me more than once, I am a partner, and the company assets are at my disposal just as much as yours. And that includes the company aircraft.'

'True, but unfortunately the jet is out of commission.'

'I don't believe you,' she said through clenched teeth. 'It was perfectly fine yesterday, when you set out to— to seduce me!'

His gaze rested on her rigidly held body, then sank to her clenched fists, and an expression of derision tautened his hard bone structure. 'Do you honestly think I would have had to fly you across a continent, at great expense to the company, to seduce you, when I could have had you in your apartment, your home, any time I chose?' he mocked as he stepped away from the door, lessening the distance between them until he towered over her like the devil she thought him to be.

Bea flushed scarlet, but she refused to be intimidated. 'That's where you're wrong, Leon. And, anyway, I don't care what you think. I want that aircraft today,' she ended furiously, only to find her shoulders gripped with fingers of steel.

'And, as I told you last night, I want you, Phoebe.' His voice was low and dangerous. 'But you obviously did not understand me correctly.'

'You can't force me to stay here; you have no right,'

she protested hotly. 'In any case I have a seat booked tomorrow with British—'

'That will be cancelled,' he interrupted, his hands biting deeper into the soft flesh of her upper arms. His nearness was an aching reminder of the night they had shared and it severely drained her confidence. 'You are not leaving here.' Thickly lashed black eyes rested inscrutably on her hot cheeks. 'I brought you here to protect you, and that is what I am going to do.'

'Protect me?' she protested heatedly. 'Is that what you call it? Invading a girl's bedroom—'

'Be careful what you say, Phoebe,' he cut in ruthlessly, 'or I will be forced to remind you just how willing a bed partner you were.' His hand touched her cheek and stroked back to tangle in her hair. 'And you will be again.'

'No,' she denied.

'Yes. We want each other, and in two weeks' time it will be legal. We will be married.'

For a second, shock held her silent, but then, as the import of his words sank in, a brittle laugh escaped her. 'What is this, Leon? An action replay of years ago, but without the supporting cast?' The memory of Selina was a constant reminder of his perfidy, even if her traitorous heart had leapt at his words. 'You must be crazy!'

'I almost was, Phoebe. Locked in darkness for days on end,' he said savagely, with seething bitterness. 'Chained by the feet like a dog. I had a lot of time to think between struggling to break free, my blood lubricating the chains, and wondering if I would die... But not any more—I learnt a valuable lesson.'

Caught in the turmoil of her own emotions, Bea had forgotten Leon's recent ordeal. Her compassionate heart touched, she studied his handsome face. His dark eyes blazed with fire but he didn't seem to see her. He was lost in the hell of his kidnap. 'What was—?'

Ruthlessly he cut across her. 'A man must protect his own against the world. I was a fool. I promised my father to look after the business and his partner, and I thought I had succeeded. Before your father died, I made him a very wealthy man, more than he ever dreamed. But what happened? Yet again, for the third time, a Stephen had to bail out a Gregoris.'

Bea listened in amazement, and with a growing sense of unease as he continued, 'You, Phoebe...' His hand felt like a steel band around her arm, and his black eyes clashed with hers, no longer unfocused, but deadly in their intensity. 'You, whom I had vowed to protect.' His other hand tightened in her hair, tilting her head back further, 'you, sweet Phoebe, ended up paying the ransom.' He dragged her up against him. 'You! Whom I should have married years ago. But instead I let you wander around at will.'

The hard contact of his body against her own attacked her senses. Bea felt the colour leave her cheeks and beneath her top a trickle of perspiration ran down between her breasts, but it was more from fear than arousal. Leon was not joking. It had bruised his male ego, being kidnapped, and it was a woman that had had to bail him out. She knew him well enough to understand how he must feel.

It did not matter to Leon that the money had been recovered. He was a very proud man, and to discover he was not invincible must have been devastating, the injury to his pride incalculable. But the fanaticism in his gaze terrified her. She lifted her free hand to his chest, hoping to pacify him in some way. Licking her dry lips nervously, she murmured, 'It wasn't your fault.'

'Oh, yes, it was. I was arrogant and headstrong. I believed the world waited on me. Now I know better, and I never want you to have to learn the same lesson. Which is why you and I are getting married, and why you are staying here. Here I can vouch for your safety.'

He meant it, Bea realised, with a sickening lurch in her stomach. The electric fence, the guards—they all made sense. But wait a minute. She told herself not to panic. He had only been free a little over a week—he couldn't have arranged everything so quickly!

'I was already in the process of improving the security here because of trouble at the partition line between Greek and Turk; it was a simple matter to hire the armed guards.'

Unfortunately, he had accurately read her mind, and his answer made sense. Dazedly she surveyed him. 'But I can't stay here.'

'Rubbish. After last night what else can you do?' And, planting a swift, hard kiss on her trembling lips, he slanted her a ruthless smile as he set her free. 'Here you will be totally secure. The guards have strict instructions—you only leave with me.' The matter settled to his satisfaction, he brushed past her and resumed his seat behind the oak desk.

'You…are…mad…' Bea said, enunciating each word slowly and clearly, as if talking to a child. 'I'm getting out of here, and you can't stop me. I'll get Anna to help me…'

Leon lounged back in the leather chair, one black brow arched sardonically, a glimmer of a grin twisting his hard mouth. 'Really, Phoebe! Anna, who brought us coffee in bed this morning? I think not. She is a very old-fashioned Greek lady. She already considers you my wife.'

'Or Lil and Bob. You can't guard the phone.' She was ʼng around for a way out.

'I have already spoken to them both. They agree with me. As a very public heiress, your security is vital. Northumbria is not known for kidnapping since the Border reiver days. But even so I have set in motion plans to have the house at Mitford secured just in case. Don't worry, darling; in a few months we will be able to go for a visit.'

'We...we... I'm not going anywhere with you. Can't you get that into your stupid head?' Bea exploded.

'I know you're staying here,' Leon whipped back in silky derision. 'Call Lil, if you like, but remember our engagement is front-page news all over Britain today, and I have already told them we're getting married. I felt it was the correct thing to do, as they have acted *in loco parentis* for so long.'

At the mention of the newspapers, Bea's mouth fell open in shocked horror. She listened to the rest and was left standing in the middle of the room, gazing at Leon with her mouth working like a goldfish. She was lost for words, and only slowly beginning to comprehend what was happening. Dear heaven, the swine had thought of everything!

The suit, the pendant he had so casually told her to wear. 'Your plan wasn't to help me escape the press, it was to help yourself,' she said, almost to herself. 'How long...?' How long had he been planning to marry her? She couldn't put her thoughts into words. Since the kidnap? Or sooner? Since her birthday...?

'I always intended marrying you one day, Phoebe, but I hadn't decided when to give up my freedom. But being kidnapped concentrates the mind marvellously, along with a few other not so nice emotions. Hence your presence here now... As for my plan, I didn't really have one—until I saw your photograph in the newspaper, in which you were wearing the pendant. I bought the ring for you originally, and I had it altered on a whim for your birthday. You gave me a golden opportunity to announce to the world we were engaged, and I took it...'

'But why?' If it was her share of the company that he wanted, he could have it. 'Leon, if this is about the business you can have it,' she said urgently, crossing to the desk where he sat lounging back in a black hide chair, looking remarkably unconcerned, while a very real fear was building in Bea's mind. 'I'll sell you my share. I don't care. You can do what you like. Just let me leave.'

Dark colour stained his bronzed skin, and a flash of naked anger lit his eyes. 'Care does not come into it, or business.' He shoved back his chair and stalked around the desk. A hard hand spun her round, his fingers exerting pressure on her narrow shoulder. 'Can't you get it into your head, Phoebe? I am going to protect you. From the minute the world knew you were wealthy, you, Phoebe, became a possible kidnap victim. The only way I can be sure you are safe is to keep you with me all the time. And the obvious way to do that is for us to get married.'

Bea backed against the edge of the desk, nervously licking her dry lips. 'What on earth are you talking about? Don't you think you should see a doctor?' He was totally serious. The days in captivity really had affected his brain. In a weird way she could understand his motivation—he was paranoid about her safety—but he didn't seem to realise the irony of the situation. By making her a prisoner in his home, he was no better than the kidnappers.

Leon cast her a hard, triumphant smile. 'No, Phoebe, but in a few weeks' time *you* may need one. Have you thought you could already be carrying my child? I don't recall that we used any protection, and I seriously doubt you are on the pill, given your virginal state.'

White as a sheet, she stared up at him. 'You ruthless bastard,' she burst out unsteadily. The thought of pregnancy had never entered her head.

His fingers tightened on her shoulder and he jerked her up against his hard, masculine body. 'Maybe, but our child won't be.' He swore roughly before his dark head bent and he brought his mouth down fiercely upon hers, forcing her soft lips to part at the possessive thrust of his tongue.

A swift, unexpected surge of need lanced through her body as his hand settled low on her back, pressing her against his hard-muscled thighs. Only when she lay supine in his arms, defeated by her own instinctive arousal to his touch, did he desert her lips to lift his dark head.

'We have been friends for years, Phoebe. Don't spoil it by fighting with me now. Everything you want or need I can provide. A beautiful home, clothes, jewels, servants, even a family. And you know we're compatible. What more do you want?' Lowering his head, he let his lips feather across hers. 'You're young, but trust me on this, Phoebe. I know... We're great in bed together; the chemistry is there. Everything will be fine.'

Bea fell back from him, shaking like a leaf. 'Fine?' He was so bloody confident, and she had never hated herself as much as she did at that moment for surrendering to his sensuous persuasion. With self-loathing came anger, and with the fear of pregnancy fresh in her mind she lashed out at him in the worst way she could think of.

'Fine?' she repeated scathingly. 'And did your mistress Selina think it was *fine* when you left her holding the baby? Is one bastard child in the family enough for you, Leon? And don't give me the "old friends" routine, or your high moral view on marriage. I don't believe you.'

He stepped back as if she had struck him, his face draining of all colour. 'Who—?'

'Who told me?' She cut across him. 'Why, Leon, I heard you,' she drawled, warming to the subject. For years it had festered in her mind, the fact that she knew of his duplicity and had never revealed it. 'I was outside on the patio when your mistress of three years told you she was pregnant. I can even quote your response: "You bitch, Selina. You did it deliberately"—or words to that effect.'

'You heard?' Releasing his breath slowly, Leon stared across the room at her. 'You knew.' He bit out a harsh laugh, his hands clenching at his sides as if he would prefer them around her throat.

'I was young, but I wasn't totally stupid,' Bea lashed back. 'I could count, Leon. Engaged nearly five months, and with a mistress two months pregnant, does not add up in any woman's book,' she said sarcastically.

Something raw and primeval flashed in his black eyes as they clashed with hers. She shivered, and a sliver of fear trickled down her spine. This was more than anger.

'You devious little bitch. You had me believing I was too old for you, and then years later you let slip that it was business; you didn't trust me. None of it was true. Your excuses were all lies,' Leon hissed. 'It was just typical female pique. You overheard a conversation and condemned me.'

'Come on, Leon,' Bea prompted cynically. The man's arrogance was incredible! Trying to make *her* out to be the guilty one! 'With good cause. A party in Newport, wasn't it?' she queried, with an arch of one delicate brow.

Leon took a step towards her and she shrank back, fear churning her stomach. But to her amazement he stopped. His face was an impenetrable mask as he stood looking down at her—a mask carved out of granite. His temper was firmly under control, Bea thought as she warily raised her eyes to his.

'If you say so, Phoebe. Who am I to argue?' His dark eyes were cold and remote. 'But it changes nothing. You will stay here. It is for your own good.'

'My own good?' she parroted. The audacity of the man was incredible!

'Yes, and we will share a bed.'

He left her standing there, speechless, and walked out of the room.

CHAPTER NINE

STUNNED by the utter finality of his last statement, Bea stood looking at the door for a long moment, hoping against hope that Leon would return, grin, and tell her it was all a joke. He'd used to like teasing her, she thought pathetically, and then cringed at her own mawkishness. That was the Leon of her childhood; the Leon who had issued his ultimatum this morning was a totally different man. Cynical and coldly dispassionate, he had told her she was staying, and that was that...

Well, he wasn't getting away with it, Bea vowed. Galvanised into action, she shot out of the study and made straight for the front door. An hour later, after walking around the perimeter wall, she was about ready to give up. When she had tried to leave, the guard on the gate had simply grinned and pretended he didn't speak English, but Bea would have bet her last penny that he did.

The midday sun was fierce, and Bea wiped her sweat-soaked brow with the back of her hand. She was just about back to where she started and had found no way out. Then she espied Anna's husband, Spiros. He was walking along, head bent, pushing a wheelbarrow full of what looked like geranium plants.

With any luck Anna might not have had a chance to tell Spiros yet about finding Bea in bed with the master. The old man could be her chance to escape. The guards would not stop him. All she had to do was persuade him to take her to the town, the market—anything, so long as she got outside.

His happy smile of greeting lifted her spirits. His English was good so she had no trouble conversing with him. She spent some time enthusing over his beautifully kept garden, but then was flattened when he congratulated her on her engagement. But, her mind working quickly, she saw a way to use his knowledge to her advantage. She accepted his congratulations with a smile, and then, confiding in him, asked if he would mind walking down to the town with her. She wanted to buy a surprise betrothal gift for Leon.

Spiros was delighted to oblige.

Tucking her bag firmly under her arm, Bea approached the entrance gates. It was going to work, she thought exultantly. Spiros spoke to the guard, explaining the situation. Like most Greek Cypriots, he was a romantic, and with a beaming smile for Bea he opened the electronically controlled gates.

She was free. Now all she had to worry about was how to give Spiros the slip, but she couldn't see it being a problem; the man was sixty if he was a day, and as a last resort she could out-run him, she thought, grinning all over her face as each step took her further away from the villa.

A car screamed around in front of them, the wheels skidding as it stopped dead, throwing up a cloud of dust. When it cleared, Bea just had time to recognise a furious Leon before he grasped her around the waist and hauled her hard against him. Her back slammed into his chest, forcing the air from her lungs, leaving her winded and choking.

But Leon ignored her and turned his attention on the hapless old man who had accompanied her, letting go in a tirade of Greek which, by the time he had finished, had Spiros looking balefully at Bea, then hanging his head and walking slowly to the car.

She felt guilty for using Spiros, but she was also mad as hell. Grabbing Leon's forearm, she tried to prise it from her waist. 'Let go of me!' she cried. 'I'm not going back with you, Leon. I don't care what you say.'

He spun her around to face him. 'Oh, but you are, Phoebe.' His deadly drawling voice sent a shiver down her spine. 'Tricking an old man.' He raised one eyebrow, his expression icy. 'A bit low, even for you.'

'How did you find out I'd left?' she demanded, staring up at him in angry frustration.

He smiled and her blood ran cold. 'The guard reports every person entering or exiting directly to me.'

Her shoulders sagged. 'I want to go home, and you can't stop me.' But her words had lost their bite. She might have guessed Leon would have back-up. He was noted for being thorough in everything he did. She suddenly felt sick. But then, looking up at him through a mist of anger and humiliation, she caught a gleam of something that looked remarkably like tenderness in his black eyes.

Their gazes met and fused. Bea was suddenly conscious of the warmth of his arm against her bare midriff. She felt herself start to tremble, her heart thudding heavily in her breast, and she swallowed hard. 'Let go of me. You have to let me go, Leon,' she whispered, desperation edging her tone.

Held in his arms, she had little or no resistance to him, and deep down she knew that if she did not escape from his disturbing influence soon, very soon, she would never leave him...

Leon's gaze burnt on her upturned face for a long moment. 'You don't mean that,' he said in a chilling, quiet voice, and, urging her forward and opening the car door, he propelled her inside. He walked to the other side and slipped in beside her. 'Never try that again,' he said flatly as he started the engine.

Too dejected to reply, Bea turned her head and looked out of the window. In a matter of minutes they were back in the villa and Anna, with a reproachful look at Bea and a scathing comment for poor Spiros, declared lunch was served.

Lunch was a silent affair, with Bea seated at Leon's side in the formal dining room, morosely pushing what she suspected was a very tasty moussaka around her plate, quite unable to eat it. The events of last night and the morning had left her feeling like a washed-out dishrag, and it was all Leon's fault. She shot him a frustrated glance. They obviously hadn't affected him at all; he was eating as if he had not touched food for weeks. 'Pig,' she muttered to herself, but he heard.

'Sorry, Phoebe? What did you say?' he enquired silkily, lifting his head and fixing her with his unsmiling gaze.

'I said you look hungry,' she compromised, not wanting to start an argument. She was too weary.

'I am a big man; I have a big appetite—as you know,' he replied, and his sensual mouth curved in a wicked smile at the sudden surge of colour in her face.

'You're a pig,' she retaliated, all thought of appeasing him vanishing at his sexual teasing.

'Ten days without food take a lot of making up,' he offered, and returned to eating, leaving Bea stricken with guilt at her callousness in forgetting his imprisonment, even as she burnt with resentment at his ability always to get the last word.

After strolling around the grounds once again, in the futile hope that she might have missed a way out the first time, Bea returned hot and exhausted to her bedroom. The sight of her suitcases, all her possessions from her London apartment, stacked in the middle of the room, did nothing for her temper. She was damned if she was going to unpack them, she swore. But was thwarted by Anna, who insisted on doing it for her...

Bea's furious resentment was still simmering when Leon joined her at the dinner table that night. She listened as he talked quietly but impersonally about the island, but she made no effort to prolong the conversation. Instead, as soon as Anna had served the dessert, she excused herself with, 'Not for me. I might get fat,' and bolted from the room.

She went to bed, taking care to lock the door behind her. The stress and strain of the past forty-eight hours had finally caught up with her. She knew that she should be making plans to escape to England. But how to face the press, her friends, her workmates, Lil and Bob, and try to explain without looking a complete and utter fool, was beyond her. Groaning, she buried her head in the pillow, and surprisingly quickly she fell asleep.

Bea awoke some time later from a beautiful, sensuous dream, in which her perfect mate was declaring his undying love, to find that a large male hand was cupping and caressing her breast. Another was tracing the line of her thigh, and a warm male mouth was nuzzling her ear.

'Leon.' She swallowed. 'How did you get in?' she asked in a voice that trembled.

'I climbed up onto the balcony, but does it matter?' he demanded, and then her lips were covered with a hard mouth and he was kissing her with a devilish sensuality that made her mind spin.

He was right again; it didn't matter... She tried to resist, but in the lingering aftermath of her dream-filled sleep her languorous body was all too eager to respond to his touch. Leon's lips left hers to seek the rosy peak of her breast, then moved lower down, touching her body with tantalising, teasing strokes and kisses. At this point she gave up the fight. She clasped her hands around his neck and offered up her body in willing surrender.

'You want me. You can't help yourself,' Leon declared with silky triumph. 'You have the face of an angel and the body of a wanton.'

She could not deny him.

Much later she lay, wide-eyed, beside him, her body boneless but her mind in turmoil. The most beautiful act between two people in the world, and all she felt was a burning shame at her helpless surrender. She eased herself up the bed and looked down at Leon. His large body was slanted across the mattress, naked and totally relaxed, his muscular chest moving gently in the even rhythm of sleep.

Her eyes lingered on his face. With his eyes closed, his firm mouth relaxed in a soft smile, he looked so much younger, and she was reminded of the first time they had kissed.

At seventeen he had swept her off her feet, and then betrayed her girlish dreams. But with the idealism of youth and enthusiasm for life she had quickly recovered, neatly slotting Leon into the Don Juan category: okay as a friend, but to be avoided as a lover. The man didn't know the meaning of the word 'commitment'.

But with the first light of dawn illuminating the night sky Bea finally admitted to herself what, deep down, she had known all along. She loved Leon. She always had and always would. But the knowledge gave her no joy.

She could do as he said. Marry him, let him protect her in his own misguided way, and glory in his lovemaking and constant companionship. Live on this paradise island. But she would be living in a fool's paradise...

Common sense told her Leon had not been his usual self since the kidnap. But eventually he would get over the trauma. Security would lose its interest for him, his burning desire to keep her safe would fade with time, and she would be left with a husband who didn't love her and not a cat in hell's chance of him staying faithful to her.

Sighing softly, Bea eased herself off the bed. She glanced at Leon as she crossed stealthily past the foot of the bed. His brow furrowed into a frown as she watched. His sleeping thoughts were no more uplifting than her waking ones, she thought sadly, strolling across to the window and staring sightlessly out.

It was no good ranting and raving at Leon, she realised. Because basically he was ill, suffering from a terrible fear of captivity and obviously feeling some kind of macho guilt that a woman had had to bail him out. Maybe there was even a scientific name for his disorder. Bea didn't know. But if she wanted to be free she had to reason with him, appeal to his better nature. Eventually he would recover his equilibrium and be the same old womanising rake he always had been. Sadly, of that she was certain...

'No, no, no!' The shout rent the air and Bea nearly jumped out of her skin.

'Leon!' She dashed back to the bed. He was groaning, muttering unintelligible sounds and words. His handsome face was contorted in agony, his long legs thrashing around the bed. 'Leon, please.'

His naked body was bathed in sweat. He was having a nightmare, that much was obvious, but Bea had no idea what to do. Tentatively she reached out her hand and stroked his fevered brow... Like a steel manacle Leon's hand closed around her wrist.

'Now I've got you, you scum,' he growled. His eyes

opened, wild and unfocused, and Bea felt herself being dragged across his mighty torso.

'Leon—Leon, please. It—'

'Phoebe?' His dark gaze settled uncertainly on the tumbled mass of her silver-blonde hair. 'Phoebe, you're not a dream?'

Putting her free hand on his chest, she pushed herself up slightly. 'You were having a nightmare, no dream.'

His big arms curled around her and he hugged her to him. 'God, I'm sorry. I didn't frighten you, did I?'

'No.' She tried to wriggle out of his embrace, but he held her firm.

'Shh, Phoebe. I've got you. You're safe now. Go back to sleep.'

'No, Leon. I don't want to be safe. I want to go home.' She felt his body tense beneath her. 'I want to see my friends, go back to work. You must understand. You can't make me a captive to your obsession. I realise the kidnap has left you with a fanatical desire for security,' she said quietly, 'but your nightmares will soon pass and you won't want to be stuck with me.'

She'd thought she was reassuring him, but she was wrong...

'I understand all right,' he snarled. 'Get to me softly, when I need your comfort, and maybe you'll win. More feminine wiles, Phoebe?'

Bea alternately begged, pleaded and yelled, trying to get Leon to see sense, but it was no good. When Anna arrived with the coffee Leon was up and dressed, and Bea was glowering at him in sick frustration.

For the next two days Leon went out of his way to try to entertain her. At breakfast the first day he suggested a trip to Limassol, and the next day a trip to the Troodos Mountains. But she rejected all his overtures, determined to ignore him.

But at night it was not so easy. The key to her bedroom door had mysteriously disappeared. Leon simply walked in and within minutes overcame her pathetic attempts at resistance. But she was fighting herself as much as him. She wanted him; she loved him. And, even though she never said the words, he was experienced enough to know she was with him all the way.

On the fifth morning, after another night as a helpless slave to his sexual expertise, Bea was drinking the coffee Anna had provided with the sheet tucked firmly around her breasts. It was stupid, she knew. Leon had seen her naked, knew every inch of her body, but she couldn't feel comfortable with him. It was not that sort of relationship. They came together in the night, like two passion-starved lovers, but in the light of day she could barely look at him.

Her coffee finished, she put the cup down on the tray by the bed and raised her head. Leon was leaning against the railings of the balcony, looking out across the bay, a coffee cup in one hand. His only covering was a white towel, slung low around his hips. Why didn't he just get dressed and leave? she thought bitterly, her blue eyes fixed on the back of his head.

He turned and their eyes met, hers burning with resentment, his distinctly mocking. 'Clutching that sheet does not hide your charms, Phoebe. I don't know why you bother.'

'Not everyone is an exhibitionist like you,' she shot back, giving his bronzed chest and muscular legs a derisory glance that did not quite come off. She gulped at the obvious bulge beneath the white towel and looked away.

'Give yourself a break, Phoebe. It's a beautiful day.' He crossed to where she sat huddled on the bed and lowered his lips to the satin softness of her shoulder.

Then he straightened up, adding, 'You must be bored, hanging around the garden all day. When I brought you here I didn't mean to stay in the villa every minute of the day.'

She glanced up at him, her blue eyes wide with surprise. The gall of the man. 'Excuse me,' she drawled, 'but that is not the impression I got when I was hauled back here the other day after barely getting a hundred yards with Spiros.'

'That was unfortunate, I admit. But Spiros, much as I admire him, is not the man to protect you.'

Bea's eyes met Leon's, and for once there was no trace of his usual mockery. And when he smiled her heart missed a beat. It was so much like the old Leon's grin. There was nothing remote about him.

'Let me take you out. We can go down into Paphos for lunch and then on to Petra tou Romiou. Legend has it that the goddess Aphrodite was born from the sea-foam. A large rock, the Rock of Aphrodite, marks the spot. It comes into sight about sixteen miles east of Paphos—not far. Bring your bathing suit; it really is a gorgeous day and you might like a swim.'

Whether it was the touch of his lips still lingering on her shoulder, whether it was simple boredom or something else...Bea heard herself agree.

They spent the rest of the morning walking around Paphos. To Bea's fascination, not more than five hundred yards from the harbour were the ruins of the Villa of Theseus.

She turned to Leon, blue eyes shining. 'I had no idea Paphos was so old, or had so many ancient ruins.'

'Like me, you mean,' Leon joked, with an indulgent smile at her vibrant face.

'Fool.' She punched him on the arm.

Later, sitting at a table outside one of the restaurants on the harbour, Bea said, 'I can't believe how lovely it all is.' Her glance went to the mighty fortress at the end of the harbour. 'Is that Roman as well?' She gestured with her hand, and turned a beaming face to Leon.

'No, Turkish, and mind your hand!' he exclaimed with a chuckle.

She followed to where his eyes were focused, and laughed out loud. A big pink pelican was attempting to snap at her waving fingers. 'What the...?'

'He's a fixture around here. The restaurant is named after him,' Leon informed her with a grin.

It was like a day out of time, Bea thought happily as she sat next to Leon in the passenger seat while he manoeuvred the car along the highway.

'How come you still drive yourself here in Cyprus, when you won't anywhere else?' Bea asked idly, recalling his outburst in the limousine in London.

Leon cast her a sidelong glance and smiled. 'Because here, as I have been trying to impress upon you, it is virtually safe. Everyone knows me, and we Cypriots look out for our own. Any crime committed around here, and the people will give the police every bit of information. A criminal rarely escapes for much more than an hour or two. It helps, of course, being a small island—nothing goes unnoticed.'

It made sense, Bea realised, but even so she couldn't see Leon being happy to remain here for ever. He was too much a man of the world. She turned her head to say so, but Leon lifted a hand and pointed ahead.

'Look.' And there in the sea was a rock.

'It's not that big,' Bea remarked, vaguely disappointed.

But once the car was parked, and the two of them had scrambled down onto the pebbly beach, Bea was oddly impressed, and somehow saddened. The birthplace of the goddess of love, she mused, glancing at Leon.

He was standing looking out to sea. That air of masculine virility which always surrounded him usually blinded her to the man inside, but with the sun glinting on his short curly hair, highlighting the grey strands, she was struck by how tired and lonely he looked. Physically he was perfect, but the horror of his imprisonment must haunt him, and, however much she might resent his treatment of her, it did not alter the fact that she loved him.

Here this place, if legend was to be believed, was where love was born, and Bea had an overwhelming urge to go to him and put her arms around him. Did it matter that he didn't love her? He was prepared to marry her, and maybe with time he might grow to love her. She had to take the chance.

She took a step towards him, prepared to tell him how she felt.

Leon looked around unexpectedly and caught her in the act of staring at him. For a long moment they simply looked into each other's eyes. Then Leon moved and his arms were around her. 'Enjoying yourself, Phoebe?' he asked tentatively.

She reached up on her tiptoes and gently put her lips to his. 'Yes,' she murmured, the kiss freely given with all the love in her heart.

'I will make you happy. I promise, Phoebe,' Leon vowed, his dark eyes gleaming golden into hers, and in that moment something intensely personal, a recognition of their need for each other, flowed between them.

'I know you will,' Bea confessed, and Leon found her lips again with his own. The ground seemed to shake beneath her feet as Leon deepened the kiss, his strong arms holding her firmly against his hard body. It was a kiss of infinite tenderness, a promise of commitment.

So it was all the more surprising when Leon yelled, 'My God!' Staring over her shoulder, he tightened his grip on her. 'Quick! Off this beach, away from the rocks. It's an earthquake!'

Bea looked down in horror; the pebbles on the beach were really moving, and as Leon dragged her along she realised he was right. The grass was moving, and the trees, and yet there was no wind. The car was shaking; two more had crashed into each other on the open road. The telephone poles shook—everything was moving.

It was like walking on jelly—impossible to know if your feet would support you. Leon found a bit of open ground and simply held her. Terrified, she buried her head in his chest and clung to him for dear life. She had no idea how long it lasted, but it seemed like hours. Then Leon took her back to the car, which was, amazingly, undamaged, and turned on the radio.

An earthquake measuring 6.3 on the Richter scale, with its epicentre in Paphos, Cyprus, had also been felt in Israel, Lebanon, Syria and Turkey. People were warned to stay as far away from buildings as possible, and to expect the aftershock.

It was a tribute to Leon's nerve and skill that they managed to get back to the villa. The house was undamaged, but part of the perimeter wall had collapsed and, worse, Spiros had been caught by the falling masonry and taken away in an ambulance to hospital.

By nightfall the first aftershock had hit, and with it came the news from the hospital that Spiros was dead.

That night would live in Bea's memory to her dying day. She sat trying to console Anna, in between drinking the coffee and brandy Leon kept plying her with. No one considered going to bed—the shock of the day's events was too severe. Only Leon was a tower of strength, doing what had to be done.

The next day the radio reported that two people were dead. A woman in Egypt, whose house had collapsed on her, and a man in Cyprus, where a wall had collapsed on him and he had suffered a fatal heart attack. Spiros. But altogether the damage was not too bad; Cyprus had been lucky. The epicentre had been twenty miles out to sea, off Paphos; if it had been under the island, the country would have been split into pieces.

Bea walked along the hall, having finally got Anna to lie down and sleep on the sofa at about eight in the morning. She didn't feel lucky; she felt like crying. She needed to see Leon. She found him in the study, leaning against the desk and talking on the telephone. As soon as she entered he put down the phone and crossed to her.

'Is Anna all right?' he asked immediately.

'She's sleeping. But all right?' Bea queried sadly. 'How can she be? Her husband is dead.' She wanted nothing more than to have Leon take her in his arms and comfort her. But instead he stepped back.

'You're right, Bea. It was a stupid comment.'

Bea. He had finally called her Bea! she thought, a smile curving her full lips. She tilted back her head and looked up at him. He had found time to change and was wearing a beautifully tailored navy suit and white shirt. No one could have guessed from his expression that he had been up all night, or that his friend had died, Bea noted. Only the black tie at his throat and the slight pallor of his skin revealed the horror of the last few hours. But there was not a flicker of emotion in his dark, shuttered gaze. No reciprocal grin...

'And, you, Bea, dare I ask?'

'Oh, I'll survive. I'm tougher than I look,' she said

chirpily, hoping to elicit a smile, but a curious sense of foreboding clutched at her heart.

'Good, good. In that case I will leave you to look after Anna while I make the arrangements for the funeral and contact a few people.' He went to walk past her.

'Don't you want breakfast, and—?'

'No. No…' Leon cut her off, avoiding her gaze and heading for the door…

She raised her hand and then dropped it again. It was as if he couldn't get away from her fast enough.

The feeling persisted all day, and that evening, when she finally saw him again and asked him what he would like for dinner, he coolly informed her he was dining out…

Bea made an omelette for herself and Anna, but the older woman could not eat. So, after seeing Anna safely to her room, Bea went to her own bedroom, and for the first time since arriving on Paphos she occupied the large bed on her own. Of Leon there was no sign.

She lay awake for hours, listening to every little sound, hoping Leon would arrive. She went over and over again in her mind the last kiss they had shared on the beach, when the earthquake had hit. She would have staked her life that Leon cared for her, but as the hours passed and his side of the bed remained empty she began to doubt.

A howling wind woke Bea from a restless sleep. She glanced towards the window; rain was lashing at the glass, threatening to break it. She picked up her wristwatch from the bedside table, and had to look twice. Nine o'clock in the morning, and yet the sky was a deep, dark grey.

Rolling out of bed, she quickly washed and dressed in jeans and a sweatshirt. Poor Anna was in no fit state to wait on anyone, and possibly Leon would want something to eat. That was if she could find him, she thought, casting a glance at the wide bed, the undisturbed pillow on his side, before dashing down to the kitchen. She need not have worried; one of the maids she had met on her arrival was obviously in control, but of Leon there was still no sign.

Bea drank some tea and ate some toast, gathering from the smattering of English the other girl possessed that Leon had taken Anna to stay with relatives and that they were now in the middle of a terrific storm.

She walked along to the lounge and gazed in awe at the view from the large windows. Water ran down from the mountains, forming mini-rivers, and the wind was uprooting plants. As she watched a huge palm tree bowed and broke. The aftermath of the earthquake, Bea presumed, and, finding a book, she curled up on the sofa and tried to read. But she couldn't concentrate. Fear for Leon consumed her.

Bea tried telling herself it was a natural fear for any-one out in such a ferocious storm. But in her heart of hearts she knew it was more. She had missed him in her bed last night, the one night more than any other when she had needed the comfort of his arms around her.

His sudden use of Bea, instead of Phoebe, should have filled her with triumph; at last he was using the name she preferred. But instead it simply added to her growing conviction that perhaps he was already tired of her...

CHAPTER TEN

THE conviction became a certainty when, at one o'clock, the maid informed her that lunch was served, and that she was off duty until six in the evening.

Bea ate a solitary meal, then wandered around the huge villa, the echo of her own footsteps the only sound to be heard. She had run the whole gamut of emotions in the past few hours, from fear for Leon's safety to anger, and finally to a fatalistic acceptance of the truth.

If Leon cared anything for her at all, he would at least have phoned to say where he was, Bea thought bitterly, wandering back into the lounge. She glanced out of the window and realised the storm had passed. A watery sun was fighting its way through the last remaining clouds. But there was no sun in Bea's heart, just a dull foreboding.

She loved Leon, and she had thought the kiss they'd shared on the beach of Aphrodite was somehow special, full of promise and a clear indication that Leon truly cared for her in the same way. But twenty-four hours later he had gone out to dinner and left her to sleep alone. And again today...

Were all women in love such fools? she wondered sadly. She shook her head in negation. The relationship was hopeless; she simply wasn't the type to be walked over by any man, and certainly not twice by the same man...Leon! She threw herself down on the sofa and, retrieving her book from the floor, she opened it, determined to read this time. But countless glances at her wristwatch played havoc with her concentration. Hope didn't die so easily...

It was three o'clock before Leon returned home.

'Good, I was hoping to find you here.' He strolled into the room. He looked as powerfully masculine as ever in an immaculate dark suit, but he also looked as if he had been up all night. The events of the past two days were reflected in the dark shadows beneath his eyes and the lines of strain etched around his firm mouth. He closed his eyes briefly, pinching the bridge of his nose.

'Where else would I be?' Bea remarked cynically, refusing to be influenced by his obvious exhaustion. 'You forbade me to leave, remember?' A tense silence followed her coldly spoken reminder, and he stared down at her with barely concealed anger in the taut line of his jaw.

'I remember. That is what I want to talk to you about,' he replied hardily, and sank down onto the armchair opposite, his long legs slightly splayed. He sat with his forearms resting on his knees, twisting his strong hands together between his thighs. His usual aura of dynamic self-assurance was no longer quite so evident.

Bea stared at his glossy bent head and waited, but the lengthening silence, the rising tension stretched her already fraught nerves, until finally she could stand it no longer. 'You missed lunch,' she blurted inanely. 'And the maid has gone home.' What she really wanted to say was, Where the hell were you last night? But she did not dare.

He bit out a harsh laugh. 'Missing lunch is the least of my troubles. I suppose I should have phoned you, but I didn't have time. Arranging a funeral for an old friend is quite a traumatic experience.'

'I understand,' she said stiffly, wanting to be convinced that this was his only reason for neglecting her.

'Do you?' He sighed. 'I think not.' And, lifting his head, he glanced across at her, black eyes clashing with wary blue. But Bea could not read a single emotion in his cold-eyed gaze.

'I had no right to bring you here, and I had no right to keep you here and force myself upon you. And if I thought an apology would do any good you'd have it... But at the very least I owe you an explanation.'

He spoke so flatly, so impersonally, Bea felt an icy hand grip her heart. 'There's no need,' she interposed. She didn't want to hear his explanation, because instinctively she knew it meant the end of their relationship.

'Yes, there is. Being kidnapped left me paranoid about safety—not just for myself but my friends too. In my conceit I presumed I knew what was best for everyone, especially you. And with the expenditure of enough money I was convinced I had succeeded. I hired chauffeurs, guards, every kind of protection I could think of. I turned this house into a fortress, and congratulated myself on doing so. But I was wrong.'

Bea's fingers curled into fists, her knuckles white. She felt sick with the dread of what was to come. She loved Leon, but it was becoming more and more obvious that he didn't care for her in anything but the most basic way. He had come to his senses, as she had known and feared he would, and was about to give her the brush-off...whichever way he worded it.

'You told me so, over and over again, and I refused to see it,' he went on wryly. 'But you were right all along. I hate to admit it, but ten days in captivity affected me more than I thought, and I panicked. I realise that now. But my deepest regret is that it took an earthquake and the death of Spiros—a death I was responsible for— to bring me to my senses—'

'It was an accident, Leon—' Bea cut in.

He rose abruptly to his feet and silenced her with a wave of his hand. 'No. You deserve to hear it all. I visited the pathologist this morning. The wall did not kill Spiros. The electric charge in the fencing, which I insisted on having installed, though not enough to kill a man, was probably enough to bring on the heart attack that did kill him.'

'You can't know that,' she protested weakly. No man should have to carry such guilt. Not even a cold-hearted devil like Leon.

'But I do. I tried to play God, to protect everyone around me, and instead nature had its revenge. The earthquake showed me quite graphically there is no such thing as absolute safety. Man might rule the world but nature rules man. I can do nothing for Spiros; it is too late. I have to accept that and get on with my life. But you I can and will set free.'

'Free?' Bea stared at him bitterly, the pain like a knife in her heart. She would never be free of Leon. She had known him all her life, and loved him for most of it. She almost told him...

But a searing memory of the last time she was here and the reason for her hasty departure—Selina, his pregnant girlfriend—froze the words in her throat. 'Thank you.' If he heard the sarcasm in her voice he did not show it.

'Yes, you're free to go. No marriage. Nothing...' His mouth twisted into a cynical smile that only confirmed her fears. 'I must have been unhinged to want to marry you—or anyone else for that matter. You're going back to London, back to your life.'

She looked at him, and through the pain common sense told her that, though she might love the man, in one aspect Leon was right. Nature ruled man. Even if by some miracle he had declared undying love for her, she knew Leon's nature far too well to ever trust him. The word 'fidelity' was not in his vocabulary.

'But I have one last request.' Leon's voice broke into her tortured thoughts. 'Would you mind waiting until tomorrow to leave? My stepmother is arriving in a couple of hours. She lived in this house for twelve years and considered Spiros a friend. She's going to attend the funeral in the morning, and then I have arranged for the company jet to take you and Tany to London tomorrow afternoon.'

Bea stared at him as if she had never seen him before. His darkly handsome face and long, lithe body, his air of casual elegance—all were there. Along with his total disregard for the feelings of others. He was insulting in his complacency. He had arranged her departure with the same ruthless efficiency that had got her here in the first place. She suddenly recognised with blinding clarity that the outcome had been inevitable from the start. It had taken an earthquake to bring Leon to his senses, but now the old Leon was back, and he didn't need her. Any last shred of hope she might have entertained was swallowed up by a burning rage at the man.

'Unless you want to stay longer? I did promise you a holiday,' Leon drawled casually.

It was Bea's turn to leap to her feet. 'My God, Leon, you have some nerve,' she yelled, staring him straight in the eye. 'I can't get away from you and off this benighted island fast enough.' Brushing past him, she ran from the room. Before he could see the tears in her eyes.

Sitting at the dinner table, with Leon at the head, Tany, his stepmother, on one side and Bea on the other, Bea had a horrible thought. She actually found herself feeling grateful to be going to a funeral in the morning. It explained her hollow-eyed, ashen-faced appearance, and excused her from having to look happy as she listened to Tany's reminiscences.

Bea couldn't help but like the woman. Tany had to be nearly sixty, but looked about forty. She was the type of woman who thought 'work' was a dirty word and expected the men in her life to look after her. Definitely lightweight, but quite witty in her own way.

She kept the dinner conversation flowing with stories of when she'd shared the villa with Leon's father and a much younger Spiros and Anna. The maid served the food, and the only sticky moment came as dessert was served and Tany turned to Bea.

'Tomorrow will be a sad day for all of us. But at least you and Leon have sorted out your differences at last. I was so glad to hear you were engaged again, even if I did have to read it in the newspaper.'

Bea was saved from answering as Tany, with a playful tap on Leon's arm, added, 'That was naughty of you, Leon. You could at least have told me first. After all, I am the only family you have. It was bad enough when the police informed me you'd been kidnapped. It seems to have done you no harm—thank God! But it was most embarrassing to find out from the media that my stepson was getting married.'

Get out of that! Bea thought with a scathing glance at his bland face. Because she had no intention of trying to explain. But with his usual charm, and lying through his teeth, in moments he had Tany believing there was no engagement, that it had all been a ruse to escape the press. The same trick he had pulled on Bea, for the opposite reason, she thought bitterly.

'Bea and I are just good friends and business colleagues. And whereas I'm used to the press hounds, poor Bea isn't. She needed to get away for a while, to let the scurrilous rumours die down. But now, what with the earthquake and the tragedy of Spiros's death, she has decided to go back to London after the funeral with you. Isn't that so?' he demanded, turning his attention to Bea, his dark eyes catching hers, willing her to agree.

Poor Bea, indeed! She was so furious that for a moment she was sorely tempted to tell Tany the truth. But what was the truth? How could she tell Tany that her stepson, the man she depended on for her income, the almighty Leon, had suffered from some kind of temporary trauma? Seducing Bea and insisting on marrying her one day, and the next, when he had recovered his senses, telling her to get lost. No, she couldn't do it...

With a last blistering look at Leon, leaving him in no doubt as to how she felt, Bea concentrated on Tany. 'Yes. Leon's right. I am going home tomorrow. Perhaps you and I can hit the shops together one day while you're in London?'

Tany enthusiastically agreed, and shortly after Bea excused herself, ostensibly to complete her packing.

Midnight, and a quiet like the grave had settled over the villa. Bea, her packing completed, left the suitcases in the dressing room and, after a quick shower, wrapped a towel sarong-style around her body and walked into the bedroom. Dropping the towel to the floor, naked, but wearing her anger like a shield, she got into bed, not expecting to sleep, but vowing she would not shed another tear over Leon.

She leaned over to turn off the light, and unexpectedly there was a light tap on the door. The door opened and Leon walked in. Bea sat up. He had changed, she noticed distractedly, into a thigh-length burgundy towelling robe, loosely tied around his waist, and revealing a vast amount of muscular hair-covered chest—he wore nothing else...

What was he trying to do? Drive her mad? She swallowed, recalling all too clearly how it felt to have that marvellous body possessing hers. She felt his eyes on her and belatedly remembered she was naked. Dragging the sheet up to her chin, she watched him with cold eyes as he approached the foot of the bed, but inside she was simmering with anger and more...

'What do you want?' she demanded curtly.

A glimmer of a smile flashed in his black eyes, and she could have kicked herself for leaving herself open to one of his sexy innuendos. But surprisingly the smile vanished as quickly as it had appeared.

'I probably won't have time to talk to you tomorrow. And I don't want you to leave without me telling you.' He hesitated, his usual poise deserting him.

'Telling me?' Bea prompted.

'Assuring you that if there are any unfortunate repercussions from our recent intimacy, then of course I will support you—marriage, money, any way you wish.'

'Unfortunate repercussions'. For a second Bea was puzzled, and then it hit her. He was talking about a child. Wide-eyed, she stared at his impassive countenance, pain searing through her and leaving in its wake a rage such as she had never known. In that moment she hated him enough to kill him. How dared he remind her? Now she knew how Selina must have felt when the devil had dismissed her pregnancy, and it gave Bea the strength to respond.

'That's very generous of you, Leon, but not necessary. I am not pregnant.' Lying like a professional, she added, 'Maybe it was the shock of the earthquake, but I can assure you, I am fine.'

'Oh.' For a fleeting moment Bea imagined she saw a flicker of disappointment in his hard-eyed gaze, but it was an illusion. 'That's all right, then,' Leon said abruptly, and, turning on his heel, he left.

Bea sank back down on the bed, pulling the sheet over her, and wished she could bury her feelings for Leon as easily as she could bury her head beneath the covers. But it was not to be.

She tossed and turned all night, going over in her mind every moment they had spent together in the past week, every kiss and caress. Every word, every argument.

Finally her own innate honesty forced her to admit that it was not all Leon's fault. Bea had to take some of the blame. She had known Leon all her life; she knew what he was like, warts and all. Immediately after the kidnap she had recognised he was not his usual self. But barely a week later, when he had offered to save her from the press by taking her on holiday to Cyprus, she had taken very little persuading. Realistically she had known, being a strong-minded woman, that once over the shock she could have easily learnt to deal with the press on her own.

To heal her wounded pride Bea could tell herself that Leon had seduced her. But in her heart of hearts she knew her own ardent response to his lovemaking had, in a way, fuelled his obsession. In fact she had begun to believe in it herself.

In the darkest hour before dawn, tears she had vowed not to shed rolled softly, silently down her cheeks as she realised that this was the saddest part of all. She had deluded herself into thinking he might love her...

The church was full to overflowing; the whole of Paphos seemed to have turned out for the funeral. Bea stood beside Tany and was glad of her company. The sound of sobbing was a constant background to the priest's sombre voice. Leon supported a distraught Anna all through the service and at the graveside.

Later, at the villa, there was nothing for Bea to do, and in the end she was relieved when, shortly after a heartbroken Anna had said goodbye and left, the limousine arrived to take herself and Tany to the airport.

Tany slid into the back seat and Bea got in beside her. The chauffeur was about to close the door as Bea glanced back at the villa for the last time, when Leon came sprinting down the steps. What now? she wondered. They had already said goodbye in front of the remaining guests, with a handshake... The handshake still rankled.

'Phoebe,' Leon said, staying the chauffeur's hand on the door. His dark eyes flashed golden. 'Phoebe, I can't let you go...'

Bea stared up at him. He was calling her Phoebe again, and for some reason the name she had always hated suddenly sounded wonderful.

'Phoebe.' He repeated her name, their eyes met and clung, and the expression in Leon's made her heart leap with hope.

'Yes?' she prompted hesitantly.

'I can't let you go...' He paused, and Bea could almost see his brain ticking over. She knew the exact moment he changed his mind. He slowly stepped back. 'Without saying...' His deep voice was wry as he went on, 'Thank you for everything, and good luck.'

'My pleasure,' she managed to respond stiffly. 'Goodbye.'

'What was all that about?' Tany asked a few minutes later as the car sped down the hillside towards Paphos.

'Nothing.' Bea dismissed Leon with a word, and prayed she could dismiss him from her heart and mind as easily. But she had not counted on the tenacity of Tany.

'I don't believe you. Leon has never run after a woman in his life except you. I know my stepson.'

Bea tried to ignore Tany, but it was hard. Half an hour into the flight to London, Tany renewed her attack in a more subtle form as they relaxed.

'The funeral today was like saying goodbye to an era,' Tany remarked quietly. 'Leon's father, Nick, and Spiros were great friends, although employer and employee, and now they're both gone. I loved Nick, you know, Bea.'

'You married him. Of course you did,' Bea said idly.

'He didn't love me. Not in the same way. Oh, he cared about me, but the love of his life was Leon's mother, Pandora. I met him three years after she had died, and he had been completely faithful to her memory.'

Her interest aroused, Bea said, 'Tell me more.' Her blue eyes rested on the still lovely face of Tany.

'I was an American on holiday with my daughter when I met Nick. It was love at first sight on my part, and I chased him unmercifully—until finally he laid his cards on the table. He said he would never love anyone again, but he was lonely. He wanted a companion, some-one to host a dinner party, to socialise with, and three years without sex was becoming difficult for a virile man like Nick.' Tany grinned. 'I soon cured his problem, and six months later we were married. I got the man I loved and a secure future for myself and my daughter, and I like to think I made Nick happy.'

'I'm sure you did.' Bea grinned back.

'Yes, but my point is, Leon is very like his father. I couldn't really be a mother to Leon, because he was already thirteen when I married Nick. Even at that age Leon was very much a young man. But I do know him extremely well. Like his father, Leon is a one-woman man.'

Bea's blue eyes sparkled humorously. 'You're joking! I hate to tell you this, Tany, but Leon has had more women than hot dinners.' And if there was an edge of cynicism in her tone, who could blame her?

'Maybe, but he has only ever loved one,' Tany responded seriously. 'And that is you, Bea.'

The coffee Bea was drinking went down the wrong way and Bea almost choked. Coughing and spluttering, she raised startled eyes to Tany's. 'What on earth gave you that idea? You couldn't be more wrong!' Bea exclaimed, red-faced.

'I'm right. Leon loves you,' Tany assured her. 'And I think you love him.' Then, diverting the conversation slightly, she continued, 'I remember, when Nick died, all the flowers, the messages of condolence, and one in a childish hand from an eleven-year-old girl. Leon asked if he could keep it, and he put it in his wallet. Odd behaviour for a grown man.'

Bea felt a flush rise in her cheeks, and with it a tiny seed of hope took root in her heart. 'Leon is odd,' she said disparagingly, but lacking her usual force.

'Maybe, but he was always fascinated by you. When he was a student in England, and spent the half-term holidays at your home, you were only four. But all his letters were full of ''little Phoebe's'' achievements—the first time you rode a pony, the first time you took a jump. Over the years I heard about all your exploits. I can remember once—oh, Leon must have been nearly thirty at the time—he came back from visiting you and your father in a foul mood. Apparently you had been reading about his women in the newspaper, and asked him about them. The poor man was mortified. He always wanted to be your knight in shining armour, and you had discovered he was as human as the next man.'

'We were good friends,' Bea said softly. And he had

been her childhood hero. Looking back, she saw the truth in Tany's comment. Leon had been angry when, as a fifteen-year-old, Bea had teased him about his women.

'And now you're lovers,' Tany declared outrageously, leaving Bea speechless. 'Don't bother to deny it. I never fell for his explanation of a pretend engagement for the benefit of the press. I'm not a fool. He wanted to marry you when you were eighteen and he still does.'

The longer Tany spoke, the more convincing she sounded to Bea.

'In a way I blame myself for your break-up three years ago. I was married for the first time at eighteen, and it was a disaster. When Leon brought you to Paphos and put a ring on your finger I thought you were too young, and I was proved correct. But you have no excuse now.'

Tany's green-eyed gaze was unwavering when it met Bea's. 'My dear, don't give up your chance of happiness for a silly argument. I watched you and Leon at dinner yesterday, and the air literally shimmered with sexual tension. Then I saw Leon going into your room last night, and I heard him leave minutes later. Whatever he's done, forget it, and grab him with both hands. Or you'll regret it for the rest of your life.'

There was no point in denying it, Bea realised. Tany was a much more astute person than Bea had given her credit for. 'Supposing I *did* care for Leon that way,' she began tentatively, 'unfortunately I'm not the sort of woman to put up with his philandering ways. And whatever you say, he *is* a womaniser. I know,' she argued, not prepared to believe that Leon was capable of being faithful. There was too much evidence to the contrary.

'Look, my dear,' Tany said with some exasperation as she leaned towards Bea and placed a hand on her arm, 'Leon is a man of thirty-five. Of course he has sowed a few wild oats in the past. But I know for a fact he was devastated when you gave him his ring back the last time, and he has barely looked at a woman since. Whatever the press say...' She leaned back and a reminiscent smile illuminated her green eyes as she continued.

'I remember the day after you left. Selina made a great play for Leon. They'd had a bit of a fling before, and she was hoping to catch him on the rebound. Leon sent her packing. But you would not believe the lengths she went to.' Leaning forward again, Tany added, 'Confidentially, the woman made a complete fool of herself. She actually tried to con him into thinking she was having his baby. How on earth she thought she would get away with it I cannot imagine. But she stuck to her story for months.'

Bea, who had been listening but not really believing until then, suddenly gave Tany all her attention.

'She finally gave up when Leon arrived in America and insisted on a DNA test. She married the father of her child—a lawyer she worked with—and by all accounts they're quite happy.'

Slumped back in her chair, Bea tried to take it all in. She had been wrong about Selina! How much more had she got wrong? For years she had tried to deny her love for Leon, convinced he was simply a man on the make. Now she was not so sure. Maybe she had been looking at Leon and seeing only what she wanted to see, ignoring his myriad kindnesses over the years. He had always been there for her when she needed him. On the death of her father. During her first foray into the workplace. In her first disastrous brush with the press. And, most important of all, he was her first lover.

'Leon is a very wealthy, personable man. There will always be women chasing him, but he is also very wily, and makes sure he is never caught—except where you are concerned. Take my advice, Bea, and when we arrive in London turn around and go straight back to him.'

'Go back to Cyprus?' Bea murmured, and amazingly the idea did not seem half bad.

'Why not? You have nothing to lose and everything to gain. I had twelve glorious years with Nick, and Leon is his father's son. You will never find another lover like a Gregoris. I know. Why do you think I've stayed a widow all these years?' She grinned. 'Once you have had the best sex, you won't be content with less.'

'You're incorrigible, Tany. Sex isn't everything,' Bea quipped.

'You can say that because you haven't had to do without it for the last ten years!'

There was no answer to that, and Bea didn't even try to give one.

Tany paused, her green eyes studying Bea's flushed face. 'Joking apart,' she said, on a serious note, 'you and Leon were meant for each other. Go back. Give him another chance and I'm willing to bet you'll never regret it. There, now I've said my last word on the subject. The rest is up to you. Think about it.'

CHAPTER ELEVEN

BEA did, for the rest of the flight. She saw Leon again, in her mind's eye, running down the steps to speak to her one last time. 'Phoebe, I can't let you go,' he had said, and for a second she had believed him. But then he had changed his mind.

She relived the nights she had spent in his arms. Could a man really make love so exquisitely without caring at all about his partner? What was it Leon had said once? 'I gave up my womanising ways the day I realised it was possible to have an erection and be bored at the same time.' Sex was new to Bea, but she knew enough to realise that Leon had been anything but bored with her.

Tany thought Leon loved Bea, but if that was so, why had he told her to leave? Guilt, maybe? He thought he had forced himself on her, when in actual fact Bea had been quite desperate in wanting him. But did he know that? No—she had never told him. Leon was a proud man. He had always looked after Bea, always been there for her. And she? What had she done? At various times she had told him he was a womaniser, a devil, not to be trusted, too old, and, to cap it all, the father of a bastard child, which she now knew to be totally untrue. Was it any wonder he was reluctant to express his true feelings? And she was no better...

Bea liked to think she was a mature adult, and as the plane touched down at Heathrow she decided to act like one. She would put her pride on the line and go back to Leon.

The decision made, she said goodbye to Tany in the airport terminal, and, in her position as a partner in Stephen-Gregoris, instructed the captain of the aircraft to refuel and return to Cyprus.

By the time she walked down the gangway at Paphos airport, in the middle of the night, she was having second thoughts. No waiting limousine this time; she wasn't expected. So she simply took a taxi.

The first shock was that the gates of the villa stood wide open, with not a guard in sight. The second was that the doors of the house were also wide open, but there was no sign of anyone. Bea paid off the taxi and walked up the steps and into the hall. She wandered through all the ground-floor rooms; the caterers had cleaned up every trace of the funeral party, and were long gone. More disturbing, there was no sign of Leon. She called his name a few times, but silence was the only response. What did she expect? It was three o'clock in the morning…

Despondently she made herself a cup of coffee in the kitchen, and pondered on what to do next. He had probably gone off with one of the funeral guests for the night—and why not? He wasn't expecting any visitors, she thought, with a tired sigh.

It was too late to return to the airport—she had dismissed the taxi anyway—and so, concluding there was nothing to be done until morning, she decided to go to bed.

After opening the door of her old room and switching on the light, she stopped. There was no longer any need to wonder where Leon was. He was stretched out, face down on the bed, cuddling the pillow Bea usually used like a teddy bear. Gently snoring, he looked heartbreakingly attractive and oddly vulnerable.

Bea walked quietly across to the side of the bed, and

stared down at Leon's sprawled body. He had shed his black suit and shirt, retaining his underpants and socks. Apart from a few incoherent ramblings, he appeared to be out for the count. With a tiny smile curving her mouth, she bent down and ran her finger over the back of his head and down the indentations of his spine. She couldn't resist the temptation.

'Leon.' She said his name softly.

'Phoebe. Phoebe, my love,' he groaned, and rolled over on the bed. His eyes fluttered open and then closed again. 'No, she's gone, left me…' he muttered, his eyes opening again.

Bea sat on the edge of the bed. He had said 'Phoebe, my love'. Perhaps there was hope for them yet.

'I haven't left you, Leon. I'm here,' she said huskily. 'I came back.' She stared down at him tenderly. Was that a trace of dried tears she saw on his cheeks? His black eyes looked up into hers, clouded with sleep, but intent.

'Is it really you, Phoebe?' he asked uncertainly. 'You're not a dream?' Dragging himself up, he lunged at her. His strong arms folded around her, pulling her across the bed, and he clasped her to his chest as though his life depended on it. 'It's true. You're here,' he murmured into her hair.

With her face pressed hard against his chest and his arms like bands of steel around her, Bea could hardly breathe. 'Please, Leon, you're suffocating me,' she managed to get out, trying to sit up.

'Oh, God! I'm sorry.' Immediately he let her go, but not completely. Pulling her up hard against his side, he kept one arm around her shoulders, and with his other hand he tilted her chin so he could look into her lovely face. 'I wouldn't hurt you for the world, Phoebe. I love you. I couldn't harm a hair of your head. Please believe me.'

Her pulse leapt violently. His breath smelt slightly of whisky, but not unpleasantly, and as her gaze met his for a few seconds she saw his heart in his eyes. The sophisticated mask he presented to the world was stripped away, his true feelings laid bare, and his dark gaze burnt with love and a touching vulnerability that warmed her to her soul.

'I believe you wouldn't deliberately hurt me,' she said in an unsteady voice. 'But...' She hesitated, about to ask the most important question of her life. 'Did you mean it when you said you loved me?' She waited, holding her breath, her blue eyes fixed on his handsome face.

'God, Phoebe! How can you doubt it? I love you, I worship and adore you. I always have, and I always will.' His deep voice shook with emotion. 'What are you trying to do to me? Do you want me to beg? Plead?'

The anguish in his tone touched her heart. 'No, Leon,' she murmured, raising her hand to cover his where it clasped her chin. Tany was right, she thought with wonder—he *did* love her. 'I simply want you to love me, as I love you.'

Caught up in his own emotions, for a moment he didn't seem to hear her. 'Because I will beg. Twice I have let you walk away, but...' And then he stopped. An incredulous expression lit his dark features. 'You said you loved me...'

Tears of joy sparkling on her long lashes, she smiled. 'Yes, Leon. I love you.'

For a moment they simply stared at each other. Then, with a low groan, Leon wrapped his arms around her and eased her down onto the bed. His dark head descended and Bea's lips parted for his kiss. But then he stopped again.

'You love me, Phoebe,' he said deeply, his fingers brushing the hair from her brow while his black eyes devoured her. 'And you will stay with me?' he asked, his deep voice hesitant, as though he was afraid to believe her completely.

'Yes,' she whispered, lifting her slender arms around his neck. She wanted to feel the warmth of his mouth. What was he waiting for?

'I hope to God you mean it, Phoebe,' he said, and with a return to his usual arrogance added, 'Because there is no way on this earth I will let you leave me a third time.' Then he covered her eager, tremulous mouth with his own.

He kissed her with an achingly tender passion which stirred her more deeply than anything had ever done before. Her arms tightened around his neck as he held her hard against him, threatening to crack her ribs, but she didn't care; she was lost in the wonder of the moment. Leon loved her... Her heart sang, and soon her whole body was singing to Leon's tune.

Clothes were discarded in wild haste. It had only been three nights apart but it felt like an eternity.

'Phoebe, I want you so badly I can't help myself,' Leon groaned as, naked, he held her beneath him. His mouth burned against her skin as he scattered kisses over her face and throat. He found the rigid peaks of her breasts and eased the ache within her with his mouth and tongue. His hands slid down over her body, his knee nudging her legs apart. 'God help me, I can't wait.'

Bea didn't want him to. She was trembling so badly she couldn't stop, and as she pressed feverish kisses to his chest, her small hands skimming over his broad frame, she remembered and relished the feel, the taste of him. 'I love you, Leon,' she cried out as he entered her. At last she was free to express herself as never before.

He moved inside her and she murmured wild avowals of love until his mouth found hers, his kiss mimicking the hunger of his great body. Locked together, fierce primeval pleasure engulfing them, they cried out their love as they reached the pinnacle together.

Bea, languorous and loved, cradled Leon's dark head on her breast, softly stroking his short hair and listening to his laboured breathing. How she loved this man... And by some miracle he loved her...

A long time later Leon raised his head. Rolling off her, he pulled the cover up over them before turning towards her, and, balancing on one elbow, he stared down into her beautiful flushed face.

'More feeling than finesse,' he said, with a rueful grin. 'But I needed you so badly. If only you knew.' With a finger he traced the delicate arch of her brow, down her small nose and around the swollen fullness of her mouth.

'Knew?' she murmured as his finger moved along the line of her jaw and up over her cheekbone, as though, like a blind man, he was learning her features by touch.

Leon sighed deeply. 'The ten days I was a captive, tied up like an animal in a cage, the only thing that kept me sane was the picture of you I held in my mind. You are the most extraordinarily lovely woman.' His hand slid lower, over the soft peaks of her breasts beneath the sheet, cupping her gently. Bea had never felt such utter contentment as she cuddled closer and listened to his deep, melodious voice.

'If I fell asleep it was your lovely face I saw, your voice I heard, your laughter. Not that I slept much,' he said bitterly. 'When I was first released, and taken to the hospital, the doctor wanted me to stay in for a week, but

I refused. Then he insisted that at the very least I should seek counselling. But I ignored all his advice.

'My one thought was to get out of Hong Kong and back to Cyprus, the one place I could legitimately call home. I was convinced I was mentally strong, and a few days in captivity was not going to affect me. I was wrong.' His hand stroked up her shoulder to the soft curve of her cheek in a tender gesture. 'You witnessed my nightmares; you knew.'

'Yes,' Bea murmured softly, encouragingly, realising he needed to talk about his experience.

'Deep down inside, I think I felt afraid. But I couldn't face the thought. Instead, I behaved like a man possessed, more arrogant than ever. I insisted on every type of security, convinced I was in control—'

'Shh, Leon, you don't need to tell me,' Bea cut in.

'Yes, yes, I do, Phoebe. I love you and I want you to understand why I behaved the way I did.' A wry smile twisted his firm mouth. 'Actually, you're the only person I can talk to about it. Locked in that hellhole for days on end, with death a very real possibility, I went over my past life and realised perhaps I could have been more generous, more kindly to a few people. I began to think it wouldn't matter if I died the next day. Except for one overwhelming regret. And that was you.'

'Me?' Bea murmured, not really sure what he was trying to say.

'Yes, Phoebe, you,' he said, and, curving his arm over her slender frame beneath the cover, he cuddled her closer to his side. 'I vowed if I got out alive I was going to have you. When I was released, and saw the photograph of you in the newspaper wearing the pendant, I suddenly saw how I could do it.'

'Just like that,' she tried to joke, but Leon was not amused.

His dark eyes burnt intensely into hers. 'No, not just like that,' he derided softly. 'My first reaction was fury that the press had discovered who you were, and named you the "Reluctant Heiress". My second reaction was that you had to be protected at all costs. The thought of you being kidnapped was too horrible to contemplate. I have no excuse for tricking you into coming to Cyprus, or for forcing you into my bed—'

'You didn't force me, Leon. I was more than willing,' Bea cut in.

'My darling Phoebe.' Leon smiled and then they were kissing each other again, until Leon raised his head. 'You're far too generous, Phoebe. I know what I did. You were right when you told me I was making you a captive to my obsession, but I wouldn't listen to you. I couldn't let you go. It took an earthquake and the death of Spiros to make me realise I was as guilty as the scum who kidnapped me. I had taken away your freedom, and I had to give it back to you...'

'I didn't want to be free of you, Leon. I used to hate it when you called me Phoebe, but on the day you called me Bea I hated that more. Because I knew it meant you didn't care about me one way or the other,' Bea told him, her eyes clouding with remembered pain.

He stared at her in shocked silence, his eyes probing hers with a burning intensity. 'Phoebe, Phoebe,' he muttered thickly. 'Not care...' He shook his dark head in amazement. 'How could you believe that for a second?'

'I did.'

Leon tightened his arm around her. 'But you must know I've loved you for years!' he exclaimed. 'I thought you were delightful as a child—my brilliant and glittering little Phoebe. But there was nothing more then, nothing sexual. But you were still hopelessly young when I realised I was falling in love with you. Fifteen, to be exact. I remember sitting in the kitchen of your home in Mitford, and you challenged me about my womanising ways, as revealed in Lil's tabloid newspaper. I was almost thirty years old and I blushed like a boy as you stood there, all long legs and totally beautiful, your flashing blue eyes laughing at me.

'I was furious. I stayed away. I told myself I couldn't possibly love a schoolgirl, and for the next couple of years I avoided you. But when I heard of your father's death I dashed to your side. As soon as I saw you I knew I'd been fooling myself...

'It was then that I made my plan. Three months to get over the worst of your grief, and then I was going to return at Easter and begin my campaign of courtship. There was no hurry, you were still far too young, but I planned to lead you gently along for a couple of years.'

Bea reached up to his face and stroked his jaw with a gentle hand, stunned but flattered by his revelations. 'Typical Leon—make a plan and go for it,' she teased.

He grinned back. 'Except it backfired. In my conceit I thought you were well protected in the wilds of Northumbria, with Bob and Lil to watch over you. A few kisses was all I planned, and then I was going to ask you to spend the summer holiday in Cyprus with me. Well chaperoned, of course, by my stepmother and sister.'

'But you asked me to marry you?' Bea interjected.

'Yes. We walked along the riverbank and I casually mentioned the young tearaways of your childhood. When you told me you were friends with one, had even dated him, I was sick with jealousy, and all my good intentions went out of the window. I decided to marry you as quickly as possible.'

'And I said yes and floated off to Cyprus with you in the summer. And then I heard Selina,' Bea said sadly.

If only she had been more mature, not so in awe of her sophisticated fiancé, she might have been able to talk to Leon at the time, instead of believing all the lies and running away.

'It was never serious between Selina and me. I'm not proud of how I behaved, though she was a willing woman when I happened to be in America, but I swear, Phoebe, it was over between Selina and me the Christmas before your father died. Whatever you may have thought you heard—'

'It's all right, I know,' Bea cut in. 'She didn't have your child.' Leon looked down at her quizzically. 'Tany told me all about Selina. But you could have told me yourself,' she scolded lightly.

'Pride stopped me, Phoebe. You had told me I was too old for you, and then, years later, it turned out that you didn't trust me. And then finally you flung Selina at me. I didn't feel like explaining myself. I wanted you to love me unconditionally.'

'I do.' Bea quickly reassured him with a quick kiss.

'Thank you, Phoebe. But as we're being honest I have to admit to a certain amount of guilt. I *did* wake up in bed with Selina at Newport. But, believe me, I don't know how. I had business to discuss with Mackenzie, and no knowledge of any party. I arrived at his home late, having flown across the Pacific from Hong Kong that morning. I was jet-lagged, the house was full of people, I had one drink and crashed out. In the morning, when I saw Selina sprawled out beside me, I leapt out of bed. I swear I never touched her.'

Bea believed him, because she wanted to. 'It doesn't matter,' she said with a smile. 'I was probably too young to get married anyway.'

'I was devastated when you gave me the ring back. I didn't make a fuss because deep down I knew you were too young. But I didn't give up hope. Instead I decided to give you time, and renew my campaign when you were twenty-one.'

Snuggling into his warm body, she pressed another kiss to his bare chest. 'Let's forget about everything,' she said huskily, running her hand along the curve of his waist. They had talked long enough.

Leon captured her hand as it slid along his thigh. 'No, Phoebe. Let me finish. As soon as I kissed you on the night of your birthday, I knew the sexual chemistry was still as hot as ever between us. I was furious when I met you in London and discovered you had a date. But I felt much more confident when I took you out to dinner, and then afterwards, in your apartment, you went up in flames in my arms. Until Margot put her oar in.'

Leon shook his head ruefully. 'I thought Margot would take care of you, but the only person she chaperoned you with was me... I watched you come home the next night from Brighton with your friends, and I saw the steaming kiss you gave that Andy boy. No sign of Margot then...'

Bea chuckled delightedly. 'You really were jealous!'

'Too right I was. The next day I kissed you in the middle of the street when we parted, determined to settle things between us once and for all the next time I was in London.'

'I remember, and Sophie, the receptionist, saw us.' Then Bea remembered something else that made her heart sink. 'Was Sophie one of your ladyfriends?' she asked bluntly.

'Sophie? What are you talking about?' Leon demanded hardily. 'I barely know the woman. She sits at the front desk, I say hello to her, end of story.'

Bea wanted to believe him, but another doubt surfaced, bringing a frown to her face.

Leon grimaced and tightened his arm around her. 'I know you don't trust me, Phoebe, but I swear to you I have never made love to any woman but you in the three years since I first asked you to be my wife.'

Leon, celibate for three years! Bea couldn't believe it! She wanted to trust him, but...

'The night I went out with Jack, I saw you leaving a restaurant with a model—the same restaurant you took me to the next night.' She couldn't keep the tremor out of her voice. She loved Leon, and she was convinced Leon loved her, but was he capable of staying faithful?

'A model?' He looked at her as if she was crazy. 'You're jealous, Phoebe,' he said with a grin. 'You have no idea how good that makes me feel.' And, swooping down, he kissed her senseless.

'You still haven't explained,' she murmured breathlessly as his muscular thighs hardened against hers.

Cupping her head in the palms of his hands, his long body spreadeagled on top of her, Leon rubbed his nose against hers in a gesture of affection. 'Remember I told you I usually stay with a friend when I'm in London. His name's Jason Wells; we went to university together. Unfortunately, on my last visit he had a ladyfriend staying with him and I had to stay at a hotel.'

Relieved to hear his friend was male, and with the warmth of his breath brushing her face, Bea wished he would just shut up and kiss her. But no such luck.

'He's a doctor at Great Ormond Street, and that night he'd been paged in the middle of his meal. His girlfriend refused to leave until she was ready. Jason is a conscientious man, so he called me and asked me to pick her up, before leaving for the hospital. By the time I arrived she had downed another bottle of champagne and was definitely the worse for wear. I had to virtually carry her out of the place, and then she tried to make a pass at me.

'Personally I think Jason could do a whole lot better. Any man with money will do for that particular lady. But it's not up to me to give him advice on his love life. God knows, mine has been a disaster until now,' he said with feeling.

'But not any more,' Bea husked throatily, and, running her hands up his back, she beamed up at him with all the love in her heart. She didn't want to discuss his past loves, so long as from now on she was his only love.

'Thank heaven!' He grinned, and brushed her lips with his own, again and again...

Bea opened one eye. 'Leon?' she asked drowsily. 'Is that you?' She could feel the warmth of a large, masculine body enfolding her.

'It'd better be!' a rough voice growled in her ear. 'Now and for ever, girl, and don't you forget it.'

She turned in his arms and stared up into his face, a soft smile curving her lips. 'Just checking,' she said with a little laugh, and twined her arms around his neck.

'Tease,' he chuckled, and rubbed his rough morning chin against her cheek. 'The quicker we're married the better. I want you to be in no doubt whatsoever that I am the only man you will ever find in your bed.'

'You haven't asked me yet.' Bea pretended to pout.

'Well, I am now.'

'Not very romantic, Leon. After all, if I'm only going to be married once, I want a *proper* proposal. Down on your knees at least.'

Leon brushed a strand of hair from her brow, his smile indulgent. 'You have had me on my knees for years. Once more won't matter.' He rolled off the bed and knelt by the side, grabbing Bea's hand in his.

'My darling Phoebe, light of my life, keeper of my heart.' Leon dramatically placed his hand over his chest, hamming it up for all he was worth. 'Will you marry me, and make me an honest man?'

Struggling to sit up, Bea burst out laughing. 'Yes! Get up, you fool, you're stark naked!' He stood up, grinning down at her.

They didn't see the door open, but the almighty crash as a tray loaded with coffee hit the marble floor had them both turning towards the door. Unfortunately Leon was still naked.

The young girl from the village screamed, put her hand to her mouth, and shot out.

Leon turned to Bea. 'Was that a yes I heard?' he asked, and fell on top of her, roaring with laughter.

'Yes, but what I want to know is, who's going to get the coffee?' Bea managed to ask, between giggles.

A long time later they made the coffee together.

BESTSELLING AUTHORS
IN THE SPOTLIGHT

.WE'RE SHINING THE SPOTLIGHT ON SIX OF OUR STARS!

Harlequin and Silhouette have selected stories from several of their bestselling authors to give you six sensational reads. These star-powered romances are bound to please!

THERE'S A PRICE TO PAY FOR STARDOM... AND IT'S LOW

$1.99 U.S.
$2.50 CAN.
Special Offer

As a special offer, these six outstanding books are available from Harlequin and Silhouette for only $1.99 in the U.S. and $2.50 in Canada. Watch for these titles:

At the Midnight Hour—**Alicia Scott**

Joshua and the Cowgirl—**Sherryl Woods**

Another Whirlwind Courtship—**Barbara Boswell**

Madeleine's Cowboy—**Kristine Rolofson**

Her Sister's Baby—**Janice Kay Johnson**

One and One Makes Three—**Muriel Jensen**

Available in March 1998
at your favorite retail outlet.

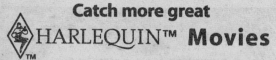 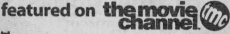